CHENJERAI HOVE

Chenjerai Hove was born in Mazvihwa, southern Zimbabwe. He is the author of several poetry anthologies and three novels, including *Bones* and *Shadows*. Hove is a teacher by profession, and was for some time Writer-in-Residence at the University of Zimbabwe. He was International Writer-in-Residence for Northern Arts, England, during part of 1995. In 1994 he was Visiting Professor at Lewis and Clark College, Portland, Oregon, USA. He lives in Harare.

CHENJERAI HOVE

ANCESTORS

PICADOR

First published 1996 by Picador

an imprint of Macmillan Publishers Ltd
25 Eccleston Place, London SW1W 9NF
and Basingstoke

Associated companies throughout the world

ISBN 0 330 34490 0

1 3 5 7 9 8 6 4 2

A CIP catalogue record for this book is available from
the British Library

Typeset by CentraCet Limited, Cambridge
Printed by Mackays of Chatham plc, Chatham, Kent

To the many silent stars of the sky,
To my mother, Jessie,
the one who remembers
but keeps silent.

Feet walk, reminding the bare soles that the destination is far-off, an unknown place at which the winds and the earth meet. Human breath tires with its history of blood and flesh. The epitaph on the grave of the traveller reads: Here lies a traveller who did not arrive, like all of us.

Acknowledgements

Many thanks to people and organizations too numerous to mention. Special thanks go to the University of Zimbabwe where I worked on part of this story while I was Writer-in-Residence. Also thanks to Lewis and Clark College for the short stint in the college which enabled me to distance myself from the daily humdrum of life back home. Thanks too to the Heinrich Böll Foundation which gave me a fellowship for a few months to spend in the Heinrich Böll Haus, the House of Silence, as visiting writers call it now.

Reveka, as she was called by the Ialites, had discovered at an early age that there was a voice within her which in spite of its being hers was nevertheless not hers at all.

From *Peasants and Masters* by Greek-Swedish novelist, Theodor Kallifatides, 1990

Part 1

The Hearer Hears of Fathers

1850 – Birth of a Deaf-and-Dumb Child

SHE FACED THE EARTH without words, this child who was born, once upon a birth. A girl without words, so unlike those who sang to their lovers the songs of the ticklings of the heart, the songs which told the birds and the wild animals that people and the life of the wild were the same, singing songs to stir the love chords of their lovers, to say, I have something which I will never know inside me. It is beautiful because it makes me move and dance. It makes me want to touch the sky even though the sky is so far away. It makes me weave patterns of joy and sadness with the silky clouds. But it also makes me want to cry with the joy and sadness of its discovery.

At birth, in a sooty hut, she did not cry. She simply forgot, they said. She was born without a history of her own. Her story would have to be told by others while she sat there and did not even nod or listen. She would see their lips and hear her story that way. They whispered, just in case the ancestors had opened her ears. Since she was deaf and dumb, there was no need for ululations welcoming a child to this world, a silent child born of a cursed woman. In the hearts of those present, it was another journey to a death, a journey which was so imminent that when they looked at the mother of the child, they saw only tears of sorrow and death. A grave in the valley.

The child did not yell loud as the other children did when they stamped their fragile feet on the harsh earth. All was silence in the sooty hut. No words, not even mumblings of words, imitations. Only faces staring at the other faces that came in and went out like sad stars after the sun has risen.

All those winds and rains, she could not name them or curse at them. She faced the earth, with its ants and anthills, in subdued silence, facing the roaring thunder and flashes of lightning with a defiant silence, the winds too, with her silence, like one who does not want to describe, or name, anything. Others would have to name the things of the earth for her, while she could not even listen.

'What is the meaning of all this?' the midwife, a woman who was spent with words, wondered, her mind gnawed away by it all.

Then the baby had growled, beast-like, a subdued beast coming into the world of strong men and women, children too running their little errands and throwing stones at each other, at the birds, at the cats and dogs which peopled their world. Only later did she growl, but the midwife knew it was too late, later than she had ever seen in her long years of welcoming new life to the huts.

of many a happy mother. She had rendered this service to many a tearful mother too, sad women who had waited all those endless seasons for a voice from within them, a voice to speak for them, saying to the world, this is my voice, a new voice that will sing for me in the world if I should die today, the voice of my memory. I have come to kindle the fire of a new homestead, not to pour water on it, the little voice of the new one said in the hearts of the mothers. This is the gift my ancestors have given to you. May your blood be happy because your veins will never die. The flow of the blood of centuries now continues to flow through me to this little piece of flesh and tender bones lying beside me under the comfort of the mud hut, the woman heard herself say, in those intense moments of childbirth, the moments when the baby leaves the mother's womb and everything is forgotten, leaving numb sleep to take over gently where once pain rested with a stubborn semi-permanence. Moments when she would gaze at the midwife and thank her with tears of joy in that joyful pain of childbirth.

But, that early morning, the midwife was astounded. Her hand clung to her breast in a permanent gesture as she, dumbfounded, stared and gazed at what the earth had given to her, this mother of a silent child. Burdens of life, she heard herself say in the silence of the early-morning dew, her words settling on the dew like dust. She felt the sting of the cool dew under the bare soles of her feet, sweet but ticklingly painful, as she walked the footpath of the village the following morning to break the news of this mysterious birth, one without a yell, empty of words as she knew them. How does she walk around the village, the cracked soles of her feet nibbling at the warm soil of the village of the ancestors, to announce this message to the village crier? How will the crier send the message to villages beyond the smoke-blue hills? Burdens, she thought. Burdens. Unmentionable burdens. In this late life, I do not deserve such thorns of the heart, she hears her own voice say, in the midst of a sadness for which her lips have no words. No, this is the harsh part of the story of my work, she thinks in her silence, memories of other births whirling and whirling in her mind and heart, the whirlwinds for which she has lived all these years with their ups and downs, life, and death too.

When the child was born, the midwife had waited patiently in a tense anxiety even her fingers could touch and feel in the numb air. Nothing was to be rewarded that day, she felt. Silence. The deep silence of a missing yell. To every silence, there was an explosive thunder, a rousing noise, a shrill voice hidden behind everything that one could ever imagine. The waiting itself became a thunder of thunders, a burning yearning. This was the time she missed the voices of children crying, mothers singing sad lullabies. Where were the village drunkards who used to pass by singing the joys and sorrows of their impending encounter with the ancestors? Where were they now when a human voice was needed to redeem this irredeemable silence?

Still no voice came. Silence, the gap between one raindrop and another, vast and distant, a pestilence of silence. The woman felt wounded by the stab of this irritating silence. What voice was it which cried in silence? she wondered. Another stillbirth? The thought startled her. No! She could not face another lonely funeral in the quietness of the valley, a subdued funeral where the mother was harshly warned never to shed a tear lest the other children hidden in the depths of her womb, the contents of which only the ancestors knew, would give up their arrival in this world of dust and rain. Why, she could scare away the other children dormantly lying in her womb, waiting to be born. In her heart, she felt another silent funeral, with women only present. She saw the stronger of the women throwing sods of dumb soil, wet, almost muddy soil, pieces of the shallow valley, closing and opening the bowels of the earth for this young baby who died without having shaken hands with the winds and the rains, the grass and the filthy soil of the earth.

The day before, she had walked about the village, sweeping the entrance to the hut of waiting. She swept the dust away, cursing anyone who dared to come near. 'Some people have bad herbs smeared on their bodies,' she said to herself. 'I don't want them near here. A mother waiting for her baby to come should not see too many monstrous eyes,' she whispered to the woman sitting inside the hut, a faint fire glowing away as if it would die, like hope when it fades away in the depth of the night. The young mother smiled and felt the movement of the baby inside her with a deep feeling of joy and contentment. It was a feeling which she could not share with anyone. Such feelings were marred by a hidden fear behind them. The joy of the new possible arrival mingled with the sadness of the unknown. It was like awaiting a stranger who announces his departure soon after arrival. When a calabash of water is carried on the head of a small girl, we can only thank the ancestors after we have drunk some of the water, the mother had heard a voice say inside her.

'Mother of my mother,' the midwife had cajoled her, 'you are only anxious because you don't know. When it happens, that withering face of yours will be one big fire of happiness.' She gave the younger mother some strength from their own ancient power. Old as she was, the woman had counted the years to her destination, the world of the ancestors. There were not many left, she had thought, her eyes glowing with a certain joy only found in those who have lived well on earth and would hope to meet the ancestors with a smile on their faces, death with the smile of a mission accomplished. No tears. No mourning as she saw herself being embraced by the arms of the ancestors on the day of her second burial.

The young woman picked up a little piece of wood and started scratching the dung-plastered floor of the hut. She was shy, and afraid of what she did not know.

And now this. Only a cave full of silence. She was like a sleepwalker who stands up in the middle of the night and walks around the village without saying a word.

It was only much later that the child growled, whimpering faintly like a dying beast. The midwife remembered, only faintly, the shrill cries of the children she had brought to this earth. The silence of this child was overwhelming. Only a growl? A growl like a puppy woken up from its sleep?

The old woman looked the other way, clasping her hands on her chest, baffled, afraid to look the younger woman in the face. Was this the strength she had shared with the younger woman? Was this the intimacy of the journey whose end none of them could tell? She glanced at the baby once more. It was a girl, this silent one. A girl. Her eyes stunned by it all, she sang in her heart of how the earth gave her this knowledge of life which had now been rendered useless when she needed its potency most. Ancestors, my ancestors, those who gave me this insight into life, the power to welcome new life unto this earth, why do you give and then take away like those harsh village lenders? Why? she wanted to know, still clasping her hands on her chest as if embracing another invisible baby, another being only she could see and share the world of the unseen with.

The smell of burning herbs in the hut told the younger woman that something was, indeed, wrong. Leaves and roots called upon to give life to those who were likely to give it up in mid-air when the dance was at its climax. She was still too weak to talk or ask the midwife what the earth was doing to her. She lay there, drained of energy as she felt the child wriggle out of her body, her rhythmic birth pangs overshadowed other pains in her body. She lay there, half of her faint, the other half alert, knowing, thinking.

The fertile woman did not even see the sooty roof

whose pattern would have normally excited her when she thought about lying in her own hut with a man to whom she had yielded the secret juices of her dark body. The man would touch her and she too would touch him, singing inside themselves those songs of endless courtship at the water well, at the river, in the forests, as they herded cattle and goats together, boys and girls searching for the only secrets of love in the hidden places of the valleys, the mountains, and the white river sands. No, not now. She waited with her mind away from her body. She did not even have a mind of her own then. The new baby had taken away everything from her hands and heart, everything which she could call her own. She only waited for the midwife to speak, to say something even if it might be a message of death. She was resigned to it.

After the midwife had stopped the blood and other waters of childbirth draining from the young mother's womb, the baby lay there in the midwife's arms, under the silent sooty roof of the hut, its eyes barely open, like a child already sleeping after suckling from the gourds of her breasts. It was as if the baby was already many days old.

The baby was still silent even after the midwife had pinched it. She wanted to startle the baby to cry, to give the mother the assurance of a voice, something for the mother's heart. She wanted to startle this silent lump of flesh out of the slumber of the womb, awaken her to her new world of thorn pricks and tears. A world in which new arrivals announced it with a cry, tears that would come out of their eyes for endless days. They always cried after this pinch, or fond slap that awoke them from the world of the womb to the world of birds and beasts, the world of people walking on two legs, the world she knew would either hate or love the baby, a doubting world where the weak grew weaker and the strong went hunting so as to show the power of their arm.

'My baby, my baby! Is it a girl or a boy?' the young woman yearns to know. 'Is it a baby like all other babies?' she insists. A baby like all other babies. She worries about the silence in the hut. She is faint in her voice, weak. Still her body does not move, numb like a log left alone in the sun. She has only this feeble power which makes her ask about her baby, the power of wanting to know, only to know and do nothing about it.

It was long before the midwife said a word to her. All the other words which the midwife spoke had been words spoken to herself, to her mind and heart as she has lived life these many years, welcoming babies to the world.

'Be quiet! Be quiet! You will spoil things. To hurry is not to arrive,' the midwife assures her. 'It's a baby. What did you think it was, a frog?' the elder woman chides the young mother.

Thus a child was born, deaf and dumb, coming to the world without a voice. The child would only speak for herself after her premature death. She arrived in the world standing on one fragile foot and then stumbled and fell hard on the unkind rock. In life, she could not speak for herself. She was one vast silence which speaks in its silence. I am only a hearer to these words, a traveller who dreams about arriving, listening to this bird lost in its flight of the night many years after Miriro died. She is now a voice that comes and goes as it wills, with no respect for any barrier. She is a dark voice full of joy and sadness, telling its story, my story, our story. I can only be a hearer shaken out of my sleep by the subdued voice of a woman of my blood, my ancestor whose tale is never told, since she was a woman. Only the story of the men, our fathers, were told. Now she sits here, in the nest of my memory, telling our story, as she lived it.

Born deaf and dumb, a baby girl, weak and fragile, wordless, what was I to do? she says into the unlistening ears. I, Mucha, the hearer of endless tales, stories to which I belong but could not assist in making, I was not part of that memory until I was born to be a mere hearer, sitting down there under the cool shade of a tree, or sleeping in the depth of the night, haunting stories which come in a voice the ears and the heart cannot resist. For, as my ears listen, it is not known how many words of the owner of words spread their mat in the ears and the heart of the hearer of a dream. I knew it.

When pain touched me, I could not cry to call for help from the other children. When joy touched me, I could not sing and dance to what my ears fed me on. I could not hear the birds singing. Birds, those wild birds which spill music into our hearts, soothing us when burdens of the heart outweigh our souls, I could not hear them. Even those lullabies which my mother sang for me, I could not hear them. They were part of that darkness which surrounded my life.

Miriro, they called me. But I could not know my name. No one knew how to tell me my name in the language of those who do not hear or speak. Miriro, the one whose voice they would have to wait for for many years, a lifetime of waiting for this girl to speak, to sing, to shout, to say something that could create a new life in the life of others.

I am the one that is yet to arrive, the one who lost her way along the long footpath to the well of life. Miriro, the bringer of anxiety into the homestead.

As I grew up, I saw eyes searching into me for what I did not know. Children, men, women, they looked at me, telling many sad stories with their anxious eyes and bodies. Some women lifted me from the ground where I sat and could not cry for attention. They simply came and lifted me in their silence. Their lips moved whenever their eyes and mine met. They said something which I could not hear and then put me down where they had picked me up as if they had picked up a lump of soil, or some rotten fruit no one would dare to eat. Then they went their way, leaving me alone, a dry leaf, alone, the bird with a broken wing which no one calls their own.

I was alone most of the time if my mother did not carry me, like a small burden, on her back. She could not sing me songs or lullabies. What was the point? she thought. The baby will not hear them. If she sang, it was the songs of her misery, to console herself, her heart bleeding to herself. Why did the ancestors give me this burden? What will I do with her the rest of her life? She will grow up, yes, but without a word from her mouth. Which man will come to this house to court her? She will work, yes, going to the water well for her mother. She will harvest crops for her mother. She will weed the fields like all the other girls, but who will love this silent one? My mother's new name became Mother-of-the-Dumb-One. It made her heart heavy from sunrise to sunset, through many nights of her nightmares.

Sometimes I saw birds flapping their wings, crossing the blue sky above my head. They turned and twisted in the sky, and I marvelled at them, wondering what they were saying to each other. They were like little feathers from my mother's hen, feathers floating up there in the sky, blown away aimlessly by the wind. The wind, the invisible wind which blew my mother's lips dry until her face told stories of disgust and shame. It was the misery of bringing on to the earth one such as me, silent, without a word from her mouth, one who could not call out her name or the name of her ancestors, the male line through which prayers were always said by the elders.

Mother came to me one day as I stood in the village playground, gazing at the birds mingled with the clouds high up in the sky. I stood there and talked with the shapes of the clouds and the colours of the birds. It was then that I saw the other children jumping up and down, their lips dancing, their skin-cloths flapping in the wind. It was some sort of celebration, a happy ending or beginning. They continued without seeing me, without thinking that I also wanted to be part of that celebration of sadness or happiness. You might have thought the birds and the clouds had escaped from the hands of the little children.

Their fathers and mothers did not bother them or order them into the world of a burdensome silence. They saw their children chasing after the butterflies and the insects, their hearts smiling at what they had brought into the world. The earth had smiled at them. They smiled back with the joy given them by their ancestors. My mother walked to where I was, her feet unsure, wondering in her heart what was happening in my heart as I watched the other children, their bodies covered with sweat, their lips dancing, their feet full of dance patterns of dust from the earth, which they kicked and tore apart at will.

I saw my mother's lips move and I smiled. Her eyes were watery, like those days when it rains and she is cooking inside the hut and the firewood is wet because the rains have been unkind. Her eyes were like that, watery and afraid. When she walked away, I followed her in my silence and saw the water from her eyes flowing nimbly down her whole face. I started crying too, thinking that she had much pain inside her. I too cried and held on to her goatskin-cloth. I held on to her and tried to assure her that I was a child, like all the others smiling in the village playground. I loved the birds which flew and danced with me in the sky. I, too, loved the clouds drifting across the sky like little feathers. Mother, when will we go to the clouds, to the world of the wind and the little feathers which run away from us and follow the clouds? The birds. When will we be birds, singing together with the birds as the other children are doing? When, mother, when?

Mother cried the whole day, and night too. I heard her sobbing, sniffing under her blankets. I heard her in my deafness. I saw her and knew the river of pain had started flowing inside her, drowning her soul.

Days and nights of growing up in pain, I felt. Mother fed me on vegetables. Children like this must not eat meat, I saw her lips say. Sunrise to sunset, my mouth opened like the mouth of a little nestling, waiting to be fed. I was brought up on *sadza* and anything else there was for children like me. I was not brought up on words and songs like the other children. Anything that could go down my throat I took, and waited for the day when I would be like all the other children.

'Silent one, where did you come from? Silent one, where did you come from?' I heard her sing many years after I had died and could look back and see the short footpath along which I had lost my way. 'This wordless child who cannot even cry,' the women said as they passed me by, wondering how my mother knew when I should be taken away to relieve myself behind the bush.

At the age when all the other children of my age were no longer lifted from the ground and spoken to in pretentious childish language, I was still being lifted up into the air, my legs frantically kicking this way and that into the air, fighting to be free. Miyiyo! Miyiyo! they said, deliberately twisting their tongues to give a certain queerness to the way they called me. The women of the village threw me back on to the hard soil and uttered some pitiful regret that the ancestors could be so cruel. This child, what will become of her? What will she become? they said, not in the silence of those who want to hide their words, but loud like lions roaring in the forest.

I was fed like a child long after the days of childhood were gone. The one who does not speak, they called me. The silent one. The one from whom words ran away.

Many years later, after I have died, I can speak. I can tell my story to all hearers. I can say all the words of the world. Do you know that I can even defeat time? My joys and sorrows cross all the rivers of time and distance, hearing voices from across generations of families and homes. I hear voices of young men and women courting before I was born. I follow women and men along the footpath of their dreams, to many places which they don't even know. You can say I am a dream now, lived by those who know how to sleep. I am a dream wafting in the air of the night, dancing with the stars, shaking their hands and nodding to the words which the stars say to me. The stories of the stars are also my stories. I live with them and they live with me. As for human beings, they are little ants in my palms. I do not crush them between my fingers, but I can take them to where I want and see them wriggle their way back to where they think their dreams ought to be taking them.

Something happened soon after I was born in my silence. Preachers of a new god arrived, with messages of a place where an angry god burned his beloved in a pit of fire. The angry god held a large forked stick in his hands, roasting the dreamers until they were ashes. He loved them so much that if they misbehaved, either in their words or in their deeds, he burnt them to ashes without pity.

Day and night, ashes upon ashes. Smoke weaving all sorts of patterns in the sky. The preachers spoke so forcefully that no one doubted they had seen the forest of fire which they talked about. Leave the evil ways of your ancestors, they said, threatening the elders of the village with death by fire.

One of the new preachers begged my mother and father to allow them to take me with them, to sacrifice me to their god. 'We will bring her up in the ways of our god,' he said, his white eyes pleading too. 'The preachers say they want to take her and bring her up in the ways which you do not understand, and they will make her their wife too, if she is a good woman, the intermediary of words had said about the words of the white men without knees.'

'Not my silent one,' mother warned them.

Father did not mind. He saw the opportunity to rid the homestead of whispers into the night. 'If they want to bring her up in their own way, let them take her,' he told my mother, his voice full of hidden joy.

'I said, not my silent one,' she cried, tears already oozing from her red eyes. Then mother took me in her arms, holding me tight, shielding me from the wind and the rain, from the eyes and desires of the strangers. Her power became greater than the power of the village and the strangers put together. Radiant power, like the sun sitting up there in the sky, telling everything that it was the difference between night and day.

'We hear from those who hear that you bring the diseases of the cattle and sexual diseases which deform the private parts of men and women,' an elder said to the white bringers of the new god. The preachers stared at each other, their strange clothes shining in the sun as the intermediary of words told them. 'Is this true what we hear from the hearers?' the elder insisted.

A gun muzzle appeared like a snake from the under-growth. It was like a witch's snake which surfaces when she is insulted.

A preacher stared at the villagers and started scribbling something in a little book. 'Heart of all evil, this is the home of evil,' the preacher with a long beard said. He was the one who had asked to take me away.

The preachers left without me. It was said the boom-booms of their guns were heard as they hunted lions and elephants, killing the giant animals, as if they were powerless rats, one after another, so easily the villagers were left in disbelief.

Miriro, they called me, the one whose voice they would have to wait for for endless seasons. I was born in the years of guns that roared with flames on their lips, killing animals and men and women. Guns of fire. This is my story, the story of the one who defeats time and distance. A dream.

'Come, child, I want to tell you the story of a dream. I am the story and the dream, a sleepwalker who only spoke when the night was done. A latecomer to dreams and words.'

Miriro takes my hand as if I am a child. She looks at the pattern of threads in my palms and then she smiles. Sometimes she smiles, at times she winces like one seeing pain in these palms. She tightens her grip and looks the other way as if ashamed to tell me what she has read in the palms of my hands. I do not know who she is and I do not want to know. To know the meaning of dreams is to look for death, my own mother had told me. She had told stories of how diviners are a haunted type, seeing ogres and ghosts in the night, for real.

'The problem is that you were born in the land of the blind, the deaf and the dumb,' Miriro says, unashamed. 'You were born when it would have been better not to be born.' She clicks her tongue in derision. I look and wonder where this journey will end, a journey with a dream for a partner. Didn't she say she was a dream, a living dream which conquers time and distance?

'You have a story within you, and I am the story. It is this story which has made you live. Not to tell it is death. A story untold is a story of death. One who has a story inside them and does not tell it means they are harbouring death in their hearts, in their souls,' Miriro, the silent one, says.

1960 – Father (the Hearer Hears)

(the stories that we hear, the victors are the only storytellers. if only the monkey could tell his own story. if only the bird could tell the story of its flight in the air. the tree, too, if it could tell its own story.

the story of our life is the story of our male blood flowing in the veins. but there is other blood flowing in our veins, not mentioned by those who know the names of things. to name is to live. a father never lies to his children. but it does not mean that he may tell all there is to be told. to omit is to lie.)

See, your father is sleepless. The Land Development Officer, the LDO, that white man who knows how to talk with the soil, says he must not grow crops just to feed the belly. You must feed the belly of the purse too, the purse. Your father has listened to the white man religiously for endless days, like a man listening to a preacher who bears a vision of the man's future. A new religion has come upon the land. The heart is caught and captured by the spell of a preacher's words. When he has been to the endless meetings with the LDO, the Land Development Officer, your father comes home, restless, like a ghost walking in broad daylight.

In the fields, he steps on the soil he has grown to love for many years. He now feels detached from it. The soil under his feet is no longer an intimate piece of earth, as it was from the time of his birth. He now despises it like an unwanted child. He fingers it and lets it filter through his fingers as if they were sieves. *Tstststs*, his tongue clicks. Pitiful sand. Sand. Sand. An ocean of sand without end, your father says to himself.

In the night, he sleeps on the mat without comfort any more. He talks to your mother about the words of the LDO and the visions of feeding the belly of the purse rather than the belly of the body.

'What do you mean, the belly of the purse? Does the LDO himself not eat?' your mother wants to know, her voice humble. She wants to know the colour of this new religion. She wants to know what crime there is in feeding the belly, the belly which the ancestors placed in front of us all so that we could remember to work to feed it and not feel ashamed. Whoever saw the belly of the purse? Whoever saw a man or woman who had eaten enough money so they did not need it any more?

'The LDO eats, but his purse is fuller than his belly,' your father retorts, obsessed by this new dream.

Belly of the purse and belly of the body. A new vision is born. Night after night, your father is restless. The echo of the voice of the LDO haunts his ears and heart everywhere he is. He has become a whispering shadow. He whispers to each of his wives. The children too overhear it. They overhear the muffled voices of the night and wonder about this man who walks in the village with the belly of the purse in front of him. A man who, because of the belly of the purse, sprinkles coins in the village playground. A man whose clothes are made of coins that make music as he walks in the village. You dream about hearing this ogre of a man walking in the night, chasing the fireflies of the night as his coins jingle and dance on his shirt. You can hear him and you marvel when he will appear. But already he appears in your eyes of the night. You are young and helpless with such images, without big dreams and visions. You see small dreams and they haunt you as if they were real. It is like that when you are a child. You dream and dream and think the dreams are there, standing in broad daylight to be real.

'I don't like the religion of the white man,' your father has always warned you as you made vain attempts to go to the white man's Sunday school. As he talks about the white man's religion, you see Noah and his disobedient children who laughed when they should not. Images fleeting through your mind, of David stealing a man's wife and sending him to be killed in the wars. 'If all of us should be drowned by the river of the white man's religion, who will brew beer for my fathers?' you hear your father's shrieky voice say as you wait for punishment by the schoolteacher because you did not go to Sunday school.

Has a new preacher, a new church, arrived in this village? The ears of the small children hear the whispers among the women, the mothers. You see the morning faces of the women wrinkled with distance. The supple dew has abandoned their feet ages ago. Their hearts do not beat any more as hearts of mothers ought to do. You see them and think that some ominous spirit has descended on this homestead. You fear to go and play outside. It is the ogres which your mother told you about who have invaded the homestead and brought this new fear in the hearts of all.

Fire burns wood to ashes and smoke. Huge trees are reduced to a patch of ashes along the footpath. Words burn hearts and minds to a valley of desires. Words in the air. Words in the heart. Words which transform the body to a huge pile of thirst. The clouds get nearer to the bleeding fingers of the hearers when words spill on their attentive ears.

Your father was not about to let go of the fiery words of the white LDO. *Makono machena*, the white bulls, as your father calls them, have been at it for many years. They know how to hunt for wealth. When you hear them tell you a piece of their mind in confidence, it is a dream they would have shared with their own people. To share wealth with them is to share the wealth of the earth with a kind-hearted people. They could have kept the secret to themselves and leave you alone to die in this poverty. Now, the young white man has talked. It is the fire in his words which matter. The fire. The fire. It is the fire which I want to eat and live by so I can also reach the lands of the skies where the white man dwells.

The words of your father go on and on like the endless winds of *Nyamavhuvhu*, the month of wild winds, in the middle of the night, in the blazing heat of the sun, in the cold winter nights when the mist envelops the hills and the valleys. You can hear his voice, cutting harshly through the night, punctuated by the sounds of the ominous night owl that sings and yearns for a death in someone's family. You are sleeping and breathing, sleeping and breathing. You are sleeping and not sleeping at the same time. You are awake throughout the night, and your father and mother will also sleep and not sleep because of this new conversation in which the LDO is always mentioned.

The night owl is hooting incessantly like an old witch impatient for your death. You hear the owl and think what it is to live out there in the rain, in the tree branches, in the *dongas* of the river, waiting for the owl to come and pick you up in the hands of its witches and bad medicine-men and -women. You think how sad it is to lie there and die in the morning dew, watched by little birds which fly past in the harsh sky, running after invisible little butterflies and insects.

The night is long and disturbed with sounds whose names or owners you do not know yet. You can no longer hear the eerie voices of your mother and father. They have been voices which merged with voices of the night owl and the jackal and the hyena. You can hear them, and you cannot hear them, voices and wails of the night. A thin voice and a thick voice drown in your dreams, in the sounds of what has always been nameless and will remain so for ever.

A whirlwind of fireflies floods your sky. A dream? Is it the one you will remember for many years? A whirlwind of fireflies floods the sky, all the maize and *rapoko* fields, flooded with a firefly the size of a hill. Many fireflies at first. You do now know which one to run after. You stand with your eyes wide open, like one seeing a python swallow a buck. There are so many of them, in the trees, on the leaves of the stubborn cotton plants which your father has tried to grow for a test. On the maize stalks. On the rooftops. Fireflies that fly and do not make any noise. Silent wings of fire. Silent bodies of tiny glowing flames.

> Firefly, firefly,
> Did your mother send you?
> Firefly, firefly,
> Where is your mother?
> Firefly, firefly,
> Where is your brother?
> Firefly, firefly,
> Where is your sister?
> Firefly, wait for me,
> My brother!

The sky is now one firefly which burns and lights the whole land. One firefly which burns and burns without its fire dying like the fire your mother lights at the fireplace.

You wake up crying. Your mother holds you in her hands and you still see the firefly in your eyes. Your mother asks you what you have seen and you mumble something which does not make sense to her. She covers you properly with the old blanket which smells of your own urine of many days. You are grateful that your mother has saved you from drowning in the river of fireflies flowing in the sky, in the winds.

'When you dream about those fireflies, don't try to catch them in your dream,' mother tells you in the morning. 'Don't try to catch them. Do you hear? They are a bad sign,' she warns you, her words not as harsh as they could be. She seems to be assuring you that dreams must be handled with care. Dreams. Mucha, a dream, a firefly that overwhelms the family, you dream.

Several conversations with the LDO later, your father does not like to use cattle manure and anthill soil to enrich his fields any more. Life changes, he argues. Life has to change, just as every year does not sit where another sat. To wait for the thin cows and angry oxen to drop a patch of brown dung before manuring my fields, it's leaving many things to chance. He laughs.

Soon, a monster machine rattles up the hill to your homestead at the beginning of the rainy season, like a rain-bird. The huge monster leaves behind it the enticing smell of a queer mixture of dust and petrol which you are not used to. You and the other children run after it, following the footpath that it has dug with its mighty hooves where you usually played, in the sand, in the dust. You run after it and abandon the cattle, shouting, singing new songs: driver, wait for me, we want to talk our problems over, wait for me, driver, don't abandon me in the forest, wait for me and sing with me the songs which your machine sings. You run, tired but not seeming to get tired, fighting on as small men do. Men who will one day grow thickets of beards on their faces. The cattle might raid a vicious man's fields, but you are sure the owner of the fields himself might also be standing somewhere on the top of an anthill, watching this monster of a machine, roaring, thundering to your father's homestead, with a trail of dark smoke and brown dust behind it. Who does not watch a thing like this arriving at a home near his home? Who does not feel it crawl up his own blood as it wriggles past anthill, tree, boulder, like a giant snake?

Everyone leaves what they are doing and runs to watch, to greet whoever it is who is moving that machine which is larger than the biggest hut. You could not compare that big machine to a donkey-cart with which you took cattle manure from the cattle pen to the fields. No. You couldn't. The one is an ant and the other is a giant mountain blowing smoke out of its back like the holy mountain which no one must climb except the white man who is not entitled to respect the shrines of your own people.

The giant machine brings loads and loads of the white man's fertilizers, all packed in white-and-yellow plastic bags too heavy for young boys and girls to lift. Strong men are called to unload the new manure as they sing their songs to celebrate their work and life too.

It is not long before the women, your mothers, ululate. They are not sure what it is that the giant machine brings, but they are certain it is not a police Land Rover which brought with it a few arrests if the dogs or the cattle or

the men had not paid taxes. Everyone knows that whenever a police Land Rover passes by the village, some
unhappy woman has been left behind, and inside there is
a weeping man in chains. Everyone knows that, man,
woman, child or dog. The women are sure about that. So
they ululate and dance a step or two of welcome to
whoever it is. Maybe they know what the monster brings.
The blue monster roaring and trudging along like an old
man whose bare feet have walked the whole land before
reaching their final destination.

It is only later that your father tells everyone about the
power of the white man's fertilizers, the magic with
which the lands of the white man are always kept green.

Excited by the smell of what comes out from the belly
of the giant machine, all the village children erupt in song
and dance.

> '*Muroora, ukatenga Rexona*
> *Muroora, unogeza mangwanani.*'

> 'Daughter-in-law, buy Rexona,
> Wash yourself in the morning!
> Daughter-in-law, buy Rexona,
> Wash in the morning.'

Or singers might sing of, oh, your mother is too poor,
why not Lifebuoy, which smells good too? The children
insult the daughters-in-law on behalf of their mothers,
provoking them to sing their own songs of insulting the
mothers-in-law, naming them all, to show them the way

home where your father will come to enquire if there is any cow or ox missing before whipping you if you happen to say yes. Sometimes you say no when you know that one or two greedy cows have been missing since midday. You want your father to count them on his own, so that you can be as surprised as he. That way he might think you were not observant enough, and so made a genuine mistake. His temper might not be as vicious as when he knows well in advance that you have committed a crime.

'Tomorrow, the cattle must graze near here, near the homestead,' you hear your father say after several seasons of using the white man's manure. Today he has taken particular interest in the cattle. He has walked into the cattle pen, touching his favourite cows and oxen, playing with the worn-out horns of the white-spotted bull, teasing it, handling it by the tail until it threatens to attack him with those horns which you, the herdboys, have secretly sharpened so the bull from your herd does not shame you every time it fights other bulls from the village. You look and wonder what it all means.

In the morning, your mother calls your name before you drive the cattle away. You go back to her hut thinking she has forgotten to give you some left-over food from last night. As you walk into the hut, the woman is busy painting the walls of the hut, decorating them with colourful soils that are pleasant to see.

'Try these,' she says, giving you new khaki shorts and a shirt.

Your heart beats with the pleasure of the smell of new clothes on your body. The smell is entrancing. You also like the shiny colour of the cloth which even important people like policemen wear. It is only your shivering fingers which delay you. Otherwise the clothes would have been on your body a long time ago. When it is all done, you look at yourself to see how they fit. There is no mirror for you to gaze at yourself. Your mother is your mirror which tells you everything. 'The shirt is a bit too big. Not to worry, you will grow with it,' bidding you farewell. 'When important visitors come, do not go near them. You never know, the white man may not like children. No one has ever seen him with children. Keep away from him,' you hear your mother warn you, the way she warns you to say away from caves where mambas and cobras abound.

In your mind it is strange that you wear new clothes to go and herd cattle. The questions in your mind continue to cause a whirlwind of confusion.

Before the sun shines on the top of your head, people start arriving at your home. Women, children, men in long trousers and coats, everyone. You see your father too, heavily dressed up in the dark suit he does not wear often. He stands there and everyone enjoys standing next to him. Chiefs with half-moon-shaped medals clinging to their necks, agricultural demonstrators riding bicycles, wayfarers who wear rags, everybody is there.

The cattle are well behaved today. They are obedient

most of the time. So you take the opportunity to go behind the anthill to relieve yourself. While sitting there in your clothes, the other herdboys shout at you to rush. They shout and laugh at the same time as if to warn you that there is a woman coming from the wrong side of the anthill. You want to finish quickly what you went to do but the body refuses. Out there on the nearby road by the river, a stream of cars already emerges. You are shocked and jump up quickly to go to the other herdboys before cleaning yourself with the bunch of leaves in your hands.

'Father says you should bring the cattle into the cattle pen now,' a voice says.

Everybody is here now, in the homestead. The LDO, the District Commissioner, the agricultural supervisor who always accompanies the LDO, the chiefs, headmen wearing everything from rebellious loincloths and ox skins to torn, over-size trousers handed down to them by their sons who work in some factory or mine. They are all here, walking in the yard, with and without shoes, gazing at the huts which our mothers have painted in many colours. They are here admiring the cattle, touching them, feeling the warmth of their skins, touching their noses as if to irritate them.

Nkosi, the District Commissioner, speaks a few words everyone understands. He speaks about loyalty to the rulers, obedience and good farming, the paying of head and cattle taxes. Then comes the LDO. He also speaks many words about good farming, throwing away the old ways and taking up new ones. Abandoning the old crops and taking up new ones. Selling the cattle with large horns and buying good cattle which are a pride to see. A good farmer must work for the belly of the purse, not for the belly of the body alone, he says, through the intermediary of languages. The people applaud, clapping hands and dancing with the impatient choir which bursts out in song. A new moon, a new sun, they have come. Open your eyes and see a new moon, a new sun. It is only a foolish man who closes his eyes when the sun rises. It is a foolish man who wants to be led along the footpath when he can see for himself.

As the two white men walk to the cattle pens, you notice the DC's skin is coarse, and rebellious-looking, worn out with the endless business of running after men and dogs in order to squeeze taxes out of them for the big Native Commissioner. But the LDO's face is smooth as a baby's. His words come out of his parted lips like water flowing from a fountain, gentle and fresh, not angry like his friend's.

Whenever the LDO mumbles something to your father, the elders move in closer so they do not miss any word from his mouth. He had refused to shake hands with them, even the outstretched hand of the chief. But when they go to the cattle pen, the LDO walks right inside, close to the cattle, touching the small horns of the bulls and the cows, patting the cows on the buttocks as if they were children, a man greeting his friends. Your father gently calls you to drive the other cattle nearer to the LDO so *nkosi* does not have to walk all over the pen filled with layers of cow dung. Fresh cow dung is smoking, green, and you fear that the clean brown shoes of the LDO might soon be smeared with dung. It is worse when the LDO, with his bare fingers, takes some of the fresh cow dung in his hands, and announces how bad the grass is for these healthy cattle. The DC, the chiefs, the headmen, everybody looks in utter amazement: a white man holding cow dung with his bare hands before the eyes of everyone?

'You are a nestling that has grown its own feathers,' the chief tells your father after the white men have left. 'If you don't fly, it's your own fault,' the helmeted chief adds. A nestling with its own feathers. You wonder in your mind who the big birds are if your father, tall as he is, can only be a nestling.

As your father's face glows with pride at the new Master Farmer's Certificate awarded him by the two white men, your heart burns to talk with your mother.

'Mother, is father a nestling?' you want to know before sleep takes you away.

'I told you not to run after the fireflies in your sleep. These dreams will drive you into madness. Leave these birds and fireflies alone,' she sternly warns you.

The night comes with dance and song, the choirs from the different villages sing insulting songs to each other. They sing and dance till the night is worn out, throwing dust in the wind, cursing the District Commissioner, the Native Commissioner, telling them to go and ask for your mother's tax first before you come here, show us the tax your dog paid before asking for ours, show us your own tax before you insult us. Bringer of bad air, where did you come from? Eater of people's liver, where did you come from? They sing without bothering that there might be detectives in the crowd, the eyes and ears of the DC. They are usually there, hiding in the crowd, sniffing around, searching for those to come and chain the following day.

Sleep does not come easily to you that night. What with all the tickling songs about the District Commissioner, about lovers who have jilted each other, about the greed of a man who cooks only when he has killed a chicken, the lazy man who does not work and waits to beg, songs about schoolteachers who impregnate schoolgirls, songs about everything in the village, outside the village, songs about everything, the mentionable and the unmentionable.

Sleep is taken away in the echoes of the songs of the choirs. Up there in the night sky of dreams, the swarm of birds invades the sky like locusts, covering it with dark wings, brightly coloured wings, dull wings. The eagles, hawks, secretary-birds, storks, *ngauzani ngauzani*, *nhengure*, the enemy of the owl. All the birds of the land are up in the sky. Your father too is one of the birds, flying away with the other birds. Flapping his wings, circling in the sky, rising and rising into the sky until he is a mere dot flying away, swallowed by the dark clouds. You call for him to come back, to return to you, not to leave you alone. But it does not help. He flies away, led by the secretary-bird which is already belching its ominous song. You are helpless. Tears ooze out of your eyes gently, and the birds go on dancing in the air, flying further and further. You hear yourself wailing as if a death has been reported in the village.

'Wake up, you!' The voice of your mother startles you. She is sad about your dreams of fireflies and nestlings. She starts to cry, holding you tightly in her arms. The warmth of her arms tells you she is worrying about you all the time you cry in your sleep.

Dreams and the blowing wind. You remember the day you followed a hornbill blown away by the wind from tree to tree, from hill to hillock, from valley to valley. You followed with pebbles in your catapult, missing the bird, grazing its feathers and thinking you are about to get it, walking a long distance to find the bird where it had perched. You sneak in through the undergrowth, stretch your catapult to hit the bird on its white belly. You have missed again. This time you feel you were almost there. Your blood boils with this near-miss. You are determined. You walk all the way across the valley, beyond the hill, yet another hill, following a bird blown by the wind. Before you know what is happening, it is dark already. You cannot find your way home. It is dark and the fireflies are already showing a little footpath to nowhere. Your heart tells you you are lost.

When you get home in the dark night, your mother looks at you with eyes that say she does not know how you were born. Her face curses her very womb and every part of your body. You start to tell her the story of the hornbill you dreamt of bringing home for her to eat. You tell her you had injured the bird and so you thought it would drop in mid-air any time. All this time, she does not listen. She merely looks at you, a dreamer lost in her small dreams, like your father, blown away by the wind, man and hornbill carried away by the wind to no destination.

1963 – Belly

You wonder where your father has been for all these weeks. Nobody has told you. All you know is he is not there. He has vanished. But one day he appears, with a small brown bag, early in the morning. Everyone welcomes him, asking him how his train journey was, if he travelled well, if he found what he had wanted to find, if there is anything interesting in the strange lands where he had gone. Everyone is gathered, listening to the tales which he brings with him. Everyone, women and children, big men who do not normally listen to folktales, crouching around the big fireplace of the open air where he, as chief, usually tries cases of those who come to argue about the unclear boundaries of their small farming plots, stolen goats or even runaway husbands and wives.

Imagine, forests and animals sitting alongside men and women, talking about the destiny of the land. Lions which come to houses and sit, listening to the conversations of the night, telling their own stories to the children, men and women. Friends of the dogs and children. People singing the songs of lions and the lions roaring back, imitating the songs of human beings, thanking everyone for living together, sharing the forests, the water, the food. Children stand up to brush the manes of the lions, brushing their teeth, playing with their tails, as you have heard in the folktales.

The land is rich, father talks on into the night. The land with grass as tall as the tallest man in the village. Father talks for the whole night about the enchanting songs of the birds of the new lands, birds whose songs no one has ever heard, songs which change into stories for those who have ears to hear. The eagles too, and the vultures, they swarm the sky, circling, reading the map of the land, seeing each grain of sand in its place, telling the little mice in the bush to keep watch before they swoop down to capture them in their hot claws. Vulture, vulture, warn me if there is buffalo nearby, the songs of the children go, in the night.

It was a strange land, he says, panting for breath. The honey-bird can lead you to where the honey is if you obey all the laws of Gotami's lands. But if you despise Gotami and defile his people's soil because of their backwardness, if you insult their trees and hills, their animals, the honey-bird too gets angry and leads you to a cave where an angry black mamba waits for you with its sharp fangs. Fangs which jut out like sharp thorns. The honey-bird knows the laws of the shrines of the land, Gotami's land, far away near the land of the Tonga people, near the waters of the Zambezi, where they say fish the size of human beings have been caught by Tonga fishermen.

If you want to know how strange this land is, how

charming, then ask those who have lived in it for so many years. They know how to behave themselves, how to talk with the ancestors of Gotami, the humble chief.

It is sad how Gotami's people were removed from those lands. One day the white man came to the chief. He drove his Land Rover through the thick, dark forest. He knew what he wanted. He came to Gotami and told him: 'This land no longer belongs to you. By next week, when the moon shines, your people and you must move beyond those smoke-blue hills in the distance. I know you will talk to me about the graves of your ancestors and their shrines. You can create other shrines in the new lands. You can take the bones of your ancestors too and re-bury them there. That is all. I have finished. If anyone wants trouble, jail and chains, they can come to the office and talk about this.'

As the white man left, soil from his footprints was taken by the most respected herbalists. They wanted the white man to come back the following day and tell them what he said was only a joke. Or to say he was dreaming because he had taken too much alcohol. How could they leave the lands which had been left to them by their ancestors, who had received them from the ancestors of their ancestors? The herbalists worked with the soil of the footprints, chanting songs to their ancestors, to other herbalists in the land, to come and rescue the land, the shrines, the graves of their ancestors, the soil in whose belly lay the very umbilical cords of the dead and the living.

The new moon brought the white man with it, this

time with guns and iron chains to see who was leading the people to rebel against the power of the white man.

Gotami's people would not dare spill blood. They had resisted spilling blood the time the Ndebele warriors came from the place of sunset and captured their women, the grain in the granaries. Everything which they wanted to take with them. Gotami himself had spoken from the ancient shrines: 'Let them take whatever they take, as long as they leave you with the land.'

Then the herbalists of the people of Gotami had dreams. They woke up one morning, took huge pots of groundnuts and left them on a fireplace without fire. When the Ndebele warriors came, they found the pots hot, the groundnuts boiling hot, steaming in thick mists of smoke. No one was there to attend to these magical pots. The surrounding bushes were quiet. No ant or lizard or bird moved. The silence of death. The silence before the stone released from a catapult hits the head of the perched bird. Silence.

The hungry warriors saw the two huge pots boiling without fire underneath them and were surprised. They stared at the pots and their eyes met, mesmerized. What is this? What does it mean? Is it a bad omen? The leader of the warriors stood there, firmly gripping his spears, and shouted to the warriors: 'Let us leave this alone. We cannot eat this. These people are witches.'

One of the warriors could not take it in, his blood already boiling with the rage of the many wars he had fought. He hurriedly stood up and asked to speak. An itching tongue must be given a chance to speak. The *induna*, leader of them all, said the man must have his say. 'This is witchcraft,' the fighter roared. 'We must destroy witchcraft wherever we find it. If they have such powerful medicine, they should have been able to stop us before we left the home of Mzilikazi. Let us eat this and see what happens. Gotami's people are cowards. They are now hiding in the caves, huddled together, children, women and men, thinking that the Ndebele warriors of Mzilikazi will be frightened by boiling pots of groundnuts. Let us eat it so that stories of our cowardice will not be sung in the songs of the drunkards of this place. Imagine, our names on the small tongues of people of Gotami, singing and dancing, deriding us in song and dance, insulting us as warriors who ran away from boiling pots, those who came all the way from the place of sunset in order to run away from two little pots. We are warriors. We vanquish both men and their medicines. I have spoken.' And the man sat down, his sweaty forehead wrinkled, angry to the bone.

With which everybody agreed. The warriors were angry now. Without waiting for the *induna*'s order, they took handfuls of the groundnuts and munched recklessly, singing the songs of their wars. They ate the whole morning, the whole afternoon, till night descended on them. But they could not finish. They ate and ate and ate. The more they ate, the more there was in the two large pots.

When night came, they were all so full that they could not walk. The warriors started dozing, lying on the bare ground like children who have overeaten. Gotami's people heard the snoring echoing in the caves where they hid and lay as still as dead logs.

By the next morning, all the warriors were dead. No one went back to tell the story of the warriors of Mzilikazi, dead in the forests of Gotami. All wiped out by two magical pots.

So the chief told them not to fight the white man. The medicine-men would see what to do. Concoctions and decoctions were mixed, tongues of lizards and tails of snakes, unheard-of plants and pieces of glittering stone, chants and incantations, all put together in pot and wind, then left there to tempt the white man to touch them. If he dared, his head would grow so big he would collapse right there in the land of Gotami, leaving the people of the land to go on with their lives, living in the land of their ancestors.

Early one morning the white man came, with bulldozers and armed men, ordering them all to get out, and the whole land was destroyed. Only the voice of the chief was heard rebuking his ancestors in harsh words, demanding to know what sin they had committed that the white man could reduce them to animals, rats and mice, little rodents which could not fight back.

That is how the people of Gotami were moved out of that land. In that land, birds, monkeys, kudu, elephants, they bathe in the river together with human beings. They listen to every conversation that goes on. The hills too, they swallow anyone who is careless with words, with language, careless enough to insult the owners of the land.

It is the land of wealth. The soil is rich, dark clay soil, rich. Plant a seed today, in two days a seedling emerges, vigorously crawling from under the soil, telling you that this is your time to feed the belly of the body as well as the belly of the purse. Only those who are careful enough to respect the shrines of the land share the destiny of wealth and prosperity. Those who care for words, for the laws of the land, the shrines. The soil feeds the belly, and the belly feeds the purse, as the LDO says.

As for those who have no respect for the angry shrines, death and insanity await them.

A man once found his whole field harvested by unknown hands in the land of Gotami. The man had worked on the holy day of the land. The owners of the land had told him, 'We have no quarrel with you. Our quarrel is with the white man who wrested the land from our hands. You have to observe our laws. Work all the other days, but the fourth day is ours to honour our ancestors and their shrines.'

'Rest and think about me on that day,' Gotami had told him.

But husband and wife whispered in each other's ears about the foolishness of the people of Gotami: 'We are people of the church of God.' They wanted to work and see what would happen. What could beat the power of their God and the Holy Spirit? They laughed as they cooked the evening meal and saw their sleeping mats waiting for them on the bare floor.

The following day, holy as it was for anyone whose foot rested on Gotami's soil, husband and wife worked all day in their field, sunrise to sunset, singing holy hymns about Christ the Conqueror of all evil, Christ the light of all darkness. They harvested as they sang. Their sweat was their life, they thought. They worked and talked about the holy words of the book of Jesus Christ, the holy Son of God. They said how wonderful God had been to them to give them this new life far away from the people who hated them and cast spells on them and their children.

Then they were tired, their limbs stiff with exhaustion. They left the fields and went home to watch the smoke of their fireplace drifting with their dreams, to the end of the earth, to the heavens.

At sunrise the following day the whole maize field was fully harvested. Maize cobs were arranged in neat piles as if a communal work party had been working the whole night. The two saw it and ran wildly to call all their neighbours to come and help them see all this. The curse of their life, an insult from the ancestors of the land. It was then that some elder's voice was heard warning them about Gotami's holy day. They should respect Gotami's laws, which were neither harsh nor hard. Did their new religion of Christ not have its holy days and shrines? he asked husband and wife.

These were the new folktales which father enchanted you with. He did not mention that you would have to name once more the rivers and hills whose names you did not know. The fruit trees, the birds, the animals, the grasses, all those names you could not find in the names of your memory. From your father's stories, the distance between the land of Gotami and the land of the ancestors was not far. The land of unending happiness, the land of the waters of the sea where fish and men shook hands and asked about each other's health.

Your father did not tell you the story of the bones of one born without words in her mouth.

2 July 1970

In the mind and heart, the words that I have always wanted to say to my father, with an urge beyond naming, they want to burst out of me, to flow like a stream down the hillside. I see them written in male blood, on the sandy footpath of the mission school where I have been sent to acquire the white man's learning and religion. The blood and the sand cling to each other, like a persistent dream in the middle of a dark night. They are the words I have shared with this woman who is a mere dream, the storyteller who tells female stories to so many deaf ears. They are stories about the female blood in me, blood that has been neglected by so many tales which father has hidden away from me.

As I wake from the sleepless night, I see the words written on the blue sky, following me like my shadow. I hear them in her voice, Miriro's, the one who is awaited, the one yet to arrive, the one who departed before she arrived.

Father

It will be a surprise for you to receive another letter soon after the last one I wrote. It is so because I feel I have to tell you a few things about my life in the past few days.

Night comes, the sun sets, and I am in the sleeping place which you can only imagine since you have never been to these parts. You remember your failed visit which my friends are still talking about? The bed I told you about? I have since changed and the prefect gave me another one because of my nights.

To put it straight, I had that horrible dream of your death again. Imagine me seeing you dying, and staring helplessly at it all. It was not just a dream of one night. It was a dream that kept coming every night. It was a dream so fresh, night after night, until the prefect decided that maybe someone put on the bed something which makes my nights miserable.

There you were, walking up the road from the fields. A man on a tractor came by and said: 'Papa, you cannot walk that long stretch. Why don't you jump on the tractor and I will drop you at home?' You were so happy about the young man's kindness. You jumped on to the tractor and he drove you towards the stream. You know the stream that passes in between our two fields? That is the one.

At the stream, the man was talking to you as he drove. He forgot to keep his eyes on the road. Then he missed the bridge and the tractor went wild. Wild like a wild beast. It crashed and you were so badly hurt, bleeding all over your face, your skull broken.

Then the funny part of it is that a woman, deaf and dumb, came over. She was watching the whole scene, not in the least worried about helping you. She just stood there, no sign of wanting to assist you. I shouted at her, trying to make her help, but she was not in the least interested. Your face covered with blood, her eyes open and clear, she was just standing there.

'I am angry.' Those were her only words, so heavy with the pain of her heart and soul.

Who is this deaf-and-dumb woman who keeps haunting my nights? Do you know her? I wish you did, so you could tell her to leave me alone. Sometimes she comes to me in the middle of the night, claiming me, wanting to take me away with her. I talk to her and she begins to cry. She cries until early in the morning, wanting to take me with her.

Greetings to everybody at home, including the little lambs which are born every day.

Your son
Mucha

My heart burns with the desire to post the letter, and I throw it into the letterbox with fresh fear. It is as if I have sent someone a snake by post. My body, in its silent language, tells me to fear. For several days I wish I had not sent the letter. Fear takes over my everything. Food is disgusting in my eyes and mouth. Friends too, like Kings, who wants to talk with me about girls and boys, about the letter my short girlfriend sent me, the other day, pleading for my latest picture, then my other girlfriend, the one I am ashamed to hear talk about, yes, that one who is five years older than me and bigger, with a breast as ripe as a mother's, the one who took me to her parents on a sports day in the city and I was so ashamed. How can I forget the episode? How she kissed me in the church when a few friends and I had visited their school and she pretended to take me around the school, then suddenly kissed me in a lonesome church, far away from the eyes of the other students?

'Has she written you these days?' Kings nudges me with naughty questions. I do not quite hear him as he goes on and on like an everlasting echo. I can only see his shadow instead of him, sitting there by my bed. 'How did you get yourself into that mess? A girlfriend who is in senior school, when you are a mere junior? Some boys are crazy, I tell you,' Kings mocks me, but I keep silent. Life has been reduced to silence. The silence of sweat. The silence of dreams and nightmares. Death.

'Listen, Kings, I am in no mood for that. Let's talk about it another day. The dream has been at me again. Whoever is sending me this dream, they are determined to kill me. Last night was the worst. I could not sleep at all. It was so real I touched the hand of the deaf-and-dumb woman. She walked right here in front of me, her face swollen with sadness. It was so frightening the prefect took me and put me up in his room, watching over me,' I tell Kings. He does not understand it. He can only clean his glasses which he is so proud of, a mark of his bookish ways.

Books are supposed to turn everyone half-blind, you know. And when you have glasses, you have some standing out there among people who know nothing about words on a page and how to absorb them into your head.

Kings, rather short and stocky, is like that, I think. He nurses the glasses whenever it suits him, to catch the eyes of any onlooker, to appear serious and educated.

'Don't let this dream thing mess you up.' I hear the distant echo of his words again.

'Actually, if it continues, I might have to leave school and go home. My mind is no longer able to settle on anything,' I tell Kings, a close friend. 'Don't tell anyone,' I confide, in a half-whisper.

'Really? Is it that bad? What letter did I see you posting? I hope you are not telling anyone that you want to leave school. I will be miserable here without you.' Kings is more serious now.

For days Kings is by my side as if I were a baby. He is more serious now. He feels pity for me but is helpless. He even asks to come and sleep with me in the same bed. He even holds my hand as we walk to class along the bare, sandy footpath.

20 July 1970

Dear child
If dreams bother you and disturb your school work, it is
better to return home. I don't know how they feed you, but

I know that at boarding school they might feed you on strange foods unfamilar to your body, like beans. If that is the case, eat less beans, or any of what they give you, and let your mind fill up with books, the aim of your being there.

Could it be that your blankets are not enough in this winter cold?

I have told your mother that all you do at school is dream about my death. She cries as if I had already died. Whoever it is you are planning my death with will one day tell everyone stories.

The rest I will speak with you about when you come for holidays.

Your father

1972 – Voices

You walk home from the bus stop where the dusty bus has abandoned you to the night full of horrors. You walk and hear your footsteps announced among the trees. You are alone in the dark world. It makes you listen, this loneliness. You listen intently to anything. There are voices of everything talking with everything. Ants talking about how they built the anthill, how they wish elephants and people and other wicked animals would not pass by, dusturbing their peace, crushing their eggs to mish-mash. Birds too are dream-singing about how the best fruit is a tomato, you thrust your beak in there once and your whole head sinks into the juice. You hear even the silent words of trees talking about how men carry axes and saws with as much pride as if humans had ever created one tree in their lives. They talk, whispering to each other. You hear and ignore, but you have heard. It is a life of noise, this. A life in which the child looks at big people making faces at each other over who said this word or that word, and for what? A life in which the silent are not so silent. Hills and caves talk as you listen. Even horses and donkeys, too, frightened though they may be, talk. They kick and run, in their frenzy, watching, screaming, giving one another the scent of life.

A woman passes by on her way to a funeral, you see it in your mind. Before she arrives at the funeral, she waits for her neighbour, who has stopped behind a bush to pass water. The woman speaks to herself. I do not have tears today, she says. Let me wait for Tauya's mother. She is the one who has a voice to cry. All these deaths, we might end up with no voices left in this village. Ah, here, Tauya's mother comes. How she walks as if going to a wedding. 'Hey, can you give me some snuff? I want to smear it on my face, drop a little of it into my eyes so tears can come out. I have no tears left since the last deaths after the tractor accident,' the woman asks of Tauya's mother.

The two women walk into the deceased's home. A shrieky voice comes out of one of them, like a thread out of a needle's eye. The other holds her face so people cannot see she is making a vain effort to shed a tear. Just a tear, a drop of salty water oozing from the eye like a half-dormant fountain.

– When I die, cry for me, please, mother, a child says. Cry for me, my dear mother. I am going to die, the child says. She has been ill, dying of malaria. Her friend died the year before, at the time of the full moon. What is death, mother? she asks.

– Don't ask such questions, the mother shouts at her. Don't talk like that.

– But what is death, mother? she insists.

Then the mother tells her that if you are dead you cannot talk with your friends. They bury you under the soil and they go away, leaving you alone. They never return to fetch you. Only witches, those who eat dead people, come and dig you out at night. When you are dead, you can't dance. You can't hear the music in the children's playground. The dead do not eat or play. They are eaten by ants and underground lizards, mosquitoes that live under the soil, anything that eats, worms.

– But mother, I don't want to die then, the girl says, her voice already faint.

I can tell you that three months later, she falls ill, and she feels she cannot speak for much longer than a few words. Cry for me, mother. Do not let them come to fetch me at night to eat me. Do not allow snakes to eat me, mother. Witches who fly in baskets and ride on the backs of hyenas. Don't let them take me away on a hyena, the child sobs.

The mother remembers as she tries to wrest a drop or two of tears at the funeral.

The night of endless, haunting dreams tells you all these stories as it walks with you along this long journey in Gotami's strange lands. You are afraid already. Fear and the night. Invisible voices in the night, in your head, in the trees. You see shapes that move as you walk, following you.

In the end, you decide to turn and ask for a place to sleep. You are not far from home, but the night tells you the fear makes it further than it is.

Sleep does not come to you. You still continue to hear voices. You overhear voices talking about your father's death. He does not want to die, they say. How can a man have a voice to defy death? He who does not want to die may not even have a voice to say so. The boy's father has been ill for many days. Disease has chosen him as the next one with whom it will show the whole village that it is still in charge of misery and tears, they say. Poor boy, what help does he think he can give? A mere boy. The man has no choice though, they say. The dying can even cling to a baby.

The next morning, you say your farewells, and the people do not offer you anything to eat so as to chase away the hunger of the morning. Strange faces meet you on the way, staring faces, gazing faces. Is it true what our ears tell us? About the death of your father? Do our ears tell us what is believable? If the story we hear is true, we will meet you there. We will follow your footsteps to see for ourselves. It is a sad thing, child, a sad thing. What will all of you do for school fees and other needs? Sad voices follow your dew-drenched feet. You hear them without hearing them. You are deaf and dumb. A zombie. A ghost.

Everyone, women, children, men with axes hanging delicately from their shoulders, children whose mouths cannot shape words properly, they ask you, shouting at the top of their voices. Even the dust of the footpath seems to ask you, demanding its pound of your heart. Is it true? Is it true? Is it true? Until your head turns and turns, whirling around into an unstoppable ghost of wind, a whirlwind.

At home, your father lies there, eaten away by disease, broken. Dying. You remember the sad face of the deaf-and-dumb woman who comes in your dreams all the time. Your father does not want to hear about her. Nobody wants to hear about the haunting woman, the one with a voice so angry she makes you lose sleep. She has now become part of you.

Your mother cries as soon as she see you. No need to ask her what pains her. It is the dreams which you have been writing about. You are here, home, alone, with voices inside you.

You sit in fear and worry, not knowing how to greet your father. A man who has run away from death on so many occasions. A man who has stood strong for so long, defying death, defying doctors and diviners. They tell you his body is no longer a body. It is only a hollow piece of flesh resembling a human body.

A voice comes again, a voice, nimble and faint. Almost silent. Do not cry, child. Do not cry. Tears have no harvest. No one ever harvests tears. You hear the voice again, like a dream.

'Father, the dream. The woman came and took me to a man who brought you medicines. Then I saw you walking in the fields once more, walking, strong, with a smile on your face,' you tell your father. He listens but his heart is away. Maybe he has heard you, maybe not. To him, it is an echo of an echo ... Your father, the flower, thought the ancestors were like a man wielding a sharp knife, a sickle, gazing at the green flower, watching and waiting for the day it would bloom. Leaves unfold. Leaf after leaf. Little branch after little branch. The flower grows and grows until it explodes with its scent of life. The land is now beautiful. Eyes can rest. Insects, too, greet the flower with the flapping of their colourful wings, dancing around it, like children around a winter fire, celebrating life in a ceremony of the seasons. The wielder of the weapon stands there, grinning, knowing in his heart that it will not be long before the dance of the insects and the little birds is brought to nought. He stands there without saying a word, his heart numb to the tickling beauty of the flower and the insects. The gentle wind blows and makes the flower look more enchanting, a piece of bewitchment like the colours of the python luring its victim before crushing its ribs.

Time was not yet ripe. You don't pluck a fruit before its time. What is the use? You pluck it and then you cannot even eat it yourself. You throw it away into the tall grass and no one will look at it. It is only the anger of the ancestors which is ripe, not the time.

If a man should fall sick, disease consuming him like a fire, it is like a break in the showers of the rain during the rainy season. The rain comes, and the plants, the little ones and the big ones, open up their arms, their fingers, their hearts. Leaves and flowers bloom. The green of the leaves takes over the forest as if the dull wood never existed. The flowers fan the wind and pat it on its back, singing praise to the coming of the rains.

Then a time comes when the rains go away to the mother of rains to take a break, to wait so the little sun can peep at the earth, making it crack like the lips of a starving child. To teach the forest that waiting is also part of the seasons. Waiting. A raindrop refuses to fall. The dew dries up. The leaves and the flowers wilt until all the eyes of the village look at the sky and curse the ancestors for being so cruel. Is it life when the ancestors give with one hand and then take away with the other? Can children of reputable ancestors be treated like a granary which is given harvests only for them to be taken away from it again? All the eyes of the village watch the sky, talking about the different shades of the colour of the blue sky every day, the feel of the wind on naked faces. Feel the air, the wind and its new freshness: doesn't that feel like rain? Everyone in the village begins to listen to *haya*, the rain-bird, singing its endless songs. The song of this bird is the song of the rains, they say. When the rains are falling every day and every night, no one listens to the lonely bird. But when the rains stop and the crops wither, everyone listens to the rain-bird. Everyone talks about the colour of the sky, the shape of the clouds, the strength of the wind from the south.

Your father was not going to die, I knew it and the other ancestors knew it. It was only a break in the downpour of the rainy season so everyone could talk about life again. To know life, you had to know death as well. Death and life are so near each other. Only the minds and hearts of the living hate to mix the two. Death and life. Fire and water. Presence and absence.

Your father lay there during his time to think. He lay there, his thoughts wandering. The insects around the flower, you the children, everyone, also waited and watched the withering flower. The children, they will call some other man father. They will be like the children of a beggar who has died and left them only misery. Their mothers are young, some of them. At my death, the young wives will be embraced by unkind hands who only want to walk where once the king walked. To touch the grass where the king's cattle once grazed. That would be talk for the drunkards and the madmen of the village. Of places far away and near.

The harsh wind of the dry season told your father that all was gone. It brought the smell of the soil of his lands to his nostrils. The earth and the wind met and took what they could take to him, a dying man who could only say his last words about everything life has been for him. He lay there withering, wilting like the little flower which was once big.

Ancestors, is it your plan that I will be the first to be

buried away from the graves of my fathers? It was this dream which took me this far. But whoever said it was wrong to dream? Dreams are not playthings for children. A long time ago, did the ancestors of my ancestors not follow the flow of the wind, dreaming stories about the lands beyond, the river Save where blood would spill until all the water was transformed into angry blood? Is that not the reason why the water of that river is holy for all the children of their children today? No one drinks that water, the blood of the dreams of the ancestors of our ancestors. Dreams. The blood of our dreams.

I too had to dream, your father says in the silence of death. This land, this land, how will it embrace me? We buried our fathers, laying them with their heads facing mountains, rivers and forests full of the stories of our ancestors. This land: how will the children lay me in my grave? The hills and mountains of our ancestors are not here. The rivers too, the rivers of our dreams, are not here. Ah, this death will be like no other death, he thinks to himself, his tongue too weak to say the words for the attendant's ears nearby. He is alone now, facing the final stroke of the knife of the ancestors. He can only think how he will settle the scores with the ancestors once he has joined them. It will be another year before he can argue with them and toss their worn-out loincloths in the air with words. It will not be long before he even knows who will perform the second burial for him so he can be brought together with his ancestors. Your father thinks all these things in the innermost mind of his heart, knowing that death has knocked on his door just as it knocked on the doors of the grass-thatched huts of his ancestors. Some of them died singing, others dancing, some hunting wild animals in the misty forests.

The day of the big wind was the worst. The trees rebelled and threw their leaves away, shaking the dust of the earth and tossing the clouds, mixing dust and cloud and leaf. The dusty soils of Gotami's lands came to his nose and said: 'We have come. Eat us, the powder of your dream. Eat us before we eat you. *Kakara kununa kudya kamwe*. The little beast gets fat by eating another little beast. The flooded river gets its water from other rivers.' He could not talk as the soil smelled rebellious, like nothing he had ever smelled before.

From a distance he heard, too, the voices of people he could not name. Life ends with a storm, they said. He should go now. He did what he came to do and now time to leave is here with us. A man who has made so much wealth should not suffer this pain. Such suffering. He should die, he heard them, their voices like faint echoes from a distance, from beyond the hills and rivers. No pity, no sorrow, in the voices, he thought in his death-like state. A man killed with words. The *coup de grâce*, in words. Two women talking, their words free as the wind. Wives tired of sleeping with the same man for all those years of happiness and suffering, years of migration from one piece of earth to the other.

Oh, how bad it is to die rich, he heard even strangers say, pained inside their hearts and souls. They had seen the faces which waited for wealth after the funeral. Faces which had no hearts to them, they whispered when no one could hear them.

Your mother looked at you without knowing what words to say. She felt it deep inside her that this man, a man she had found so young and poor, had brought so many other people around him. They were careless people who did not care for his soul, she had thought, hearing all the words and voices which spoke about wealth and the belly of their own purses. She did not have the words, your mother, to say what was inside her. She just stared, a mere visitor to this new kingdom of death, where no one wanted their words to go beyond the mouth of the grave.

Bring his favourite clothes and blankets, the women had whispered, looking at death in the face. Bring them now, now! they shouted in subdued whispers. Their festival was near, you heard yourself say, angry. The festival. It was a festival of death to those who were onlookers, dreamers, like you.

Even Mishek, the careless nephew, talked about strangers who arrive and become familiar, then depart, not in the way they had arrived. Life and death of a traveller. The fall of a kingdom which rose and fell like a tree growing in the wild. Sandals wear out, Mishek said. My sandals wear out and die. He was day-dreaming, accepting death. Animals, angels and ghosts, how do they end, if not in death? Mishek went on day after day, into the night, resigned to this imminent death. Life so close to its destination, its new departure. The traveller almost there, his feet touching the streams of his destination. Mishek – you remember the stories your father told everyone about him. He went to extract him, years back, from a life of petty crime, village fights and recklessness, to bring into his blood the rhythm of work on the new farm in Gotami's lands.

Your father had travelled many days and nights in search of Mishek, searching for a man with no particular destination in life. Son of my sister, your father had said to Mishek, instead of wasting your days in drink and women here, come, let us work the rich soils of these new lands together. You will be my hand and I will be your keeper, your heart, your everything, he pleaded with Mishek.

Mishek stared at your father and smiled. He hated to see people pleading for anything. They become children when they plead, he said, speaking of how men losing a fist fight pleaded with him, their eyes like the eyes of corpses which died with fear in their hearts. He could not remember ever hearing such words from his uncle. Calm and soothing words which gave him the assurance that at least his uncle thinks there is something in me worth salvaging.

'I will think about it.' Mishek puffed at his newspaper-rolled cigarette. Equipped only with the smoke from his mouth and nostrils, Mishek had puffed into the air, describing intricate patterns in the air, hills and valleys, ghosts and trees. Your father saw it and smiled in acknowledgement, feeling a certain hidden elation in this small achievement. It was not long before they shared the paper-rolled cigarette. One blood, one smoke.

After seven years, Mishek had decided to follow his uncle to the lands of the *maroro* fruit, where the fruit grew with your heart, where hares and buck grazed behind your hut, waiting to be slaughtered for the day's meal. Where everything was there with you, waiting and being waited for.

It had not taken long for his wife, his half-blind mother and half-naked children to pack their few belongings and take the next bus. For ever to follow the dreams of a new land, with rich soils and a fresh wildness which made people live longer and happier lives, the words of his uncle had said. Never again to return to the bare lands of poverty and misery, Mishek thought, as he shook the coarse and dusty hands of all his relatives in farewell.

The villagers remembered Mishek as a man who did anything that the heart desired. Mashiri, they nicknamed him. It was after he had sold a man colourful birds that they gave him the name. The-Seller-of-Wild-Birds. He had sold wild birds to a man without catching them. Everyone talked about Mishek's bird adventures, and others.

You know this man, they said, he can sell you even the shirt he is wearing. 'I will deliver this shirt to you tomorrow. Let us have a drink, son of our people. Let us have a drink from the money you gave me. Life must be enjoyed while it lasts. The dead are foolish not to have enjoyed life before the ants ate them. This is a big proverb which our elders left us. The problem is that in our foolishness we never listen to the sayings of our elders. We are deaf, and when misfortunes befall us, we think the ancestors are turning their backs on us.' They heard the echoes of Mishek's voice for a long time after his uncle had taken him away to the land of dreams that did not turn into nightmares.

Then drinks and drinks and drinks from this man who is the salt of the earth, Seller-of-Wild-Birds. The skies have opened. Heavy drops fall on the throats of the villagers. The seven-day brew tells everyone that Mishek is a good drummer, and a steady drinker too. He makes the drums speak in a language never before heard in these parts. Drums cough and sneeze in his hands. He makes every man and woman think of the lovers they did not marry.

> The one whose voice,
> like the white man's metallic whistle,
> why did I not marry her?
> The one whose breasts,
> erect like the horns of a small bull,
> why did she vanish from my eyes?
> Large breast on mother-in-law's chest,
> why did you choose the mother-in-law's chest,
> running away from my wife?
> The woman who turned muddy water into tea,
> why did my eyes lose her
> as she entered the forest?
> The one whose mother was so kind to me,

why did her father hate me?
Heavens,
did the ancestors make me remain for this?
Heavens,
did the sky look at this,
remaining silent?
Hearers of this land,
your ears should burst.
Seers of this land,
your eyes don't see what I see.

The villagers remembered Mishek, the prophet of the drum. He bewitches them with his palms as they dance on the ox skin stretched on the drum. Then his tongue completes the story, making everything look so easy from day to day.

And when the villagers leave to go home after the beer, Mishek says to the man, in whispered intimacies: Thanks for the drink, son of our people. May the ancestors give us more people like you so the land can be livable. In drink, we share the laughter of the joys and sorrows of life. In drink, your ancestors and mine shake hands and say: See, our children know how to share the earth.

The village drunks nod in agreement, shaking hands with the buyer of the shirt he will never wear. Life must be lived with friends alone, not enemies. Those that share the gourd of life, may they inhabit this village. Earth, earth, earth, learn to hesitate to take the good people from the earth. The drunks stagger home, in various states of drunkenness, mumbling, singing at times, cursing the earth, cursing everyone, the young and the old, hills and rivers which harbour witches and hyenas, the vicious birds like *nhengure* which tear off the feathers of the others to amuse themselves. Cursing the headman for his stingy ways when he gives land to the villagers. *Sabhuku, meso amai vako, Sabhuku meso amai vako.* Insulting the ugliness of the headman's mother's eyes.

Three days later, the buyer of the shirt remembers Mishek. But Mishek only remembers how the kind man buys beer as if the frothy liquid is about to vanish from the village. Did I not thank you in front of all who looked at us and enjoyed the fruits of our friendship? Did I not praise the wise counsel you received from the wise men of your people? Ask Marunda, the man who drank until he shat in his trousers, did I ever promise you a shirt? And to think that I could sell you a shirt I was wearing! Mishek laughs loud and leans on the thin tree trunk of his home, his face and heart contented.

Mishek escapes in his laughter. Even the headman remembers how Mishek sets fire to the wild grass and the bush, then goes to the headmen to tell stories about how bad some village smokers are when they buy the cigarettes from the white man's shop. Everyone remembers how anyone who lent money to Mishek will be happy with the news and stories of how Mishek will not pay him back. Nobody holds a grudge against him for that, even those whose drums he played the whole night and then blamed for poor craftsmanship, they only look and swallow dusty saliva.

In the year of pain, talkers did not need the ears of

hearers to hear them. They just talked in streams of words which did not need to be hidden in proverbs.

A few months later, eyes see your father walking. They are not ashamed to cry hot tears, to blame themselves. They look and thank their ancestors for allowing them to see this walking miracle. Ancestors, come and help us to see this. See this with us. Strange happenings must be seen in the presence of those who have strength, they mourn, before passing suspicious greetings to your father.

1972 – Father

You, a mere boy, watch your father as he paces up and down the lands of his dreams. His bright moments are measured in the greenness of the crops, a man of the dark soil, black soil from which grew dreams or nightmares if the rains did not fall. He is a ravisher of fat oxen too, and cows with calves, mooing.

These are bright moments. He is a man of the soil. In those years of the search, whenever he returned from his travels, he was out of breath with the stories of elephants and lions in this land of Gotami. Together with other dreamers, he had visited the new lands which the white man had taken away from Gotami's people. You cannot buy the large farmlands of the white man. You are still infants of farming, mere infants. Buy these lands from which we sent away the people of Gotami, the people who would not put up a fight for their lands. They are your lands now, the white man had said.

'The land of our dreams,' your father said as you sat around the fire, listening to the entrancing stories of lions and elephants talking with vultures and the honey-bird. In the land of your birth, there was nothing to fear except a few thin snakes slithering through the bush, afraid of the eagle and the hungry hawk. There were also men hired to hunt for small boys and girls, especially first- or last-borns. Those were good ingredients of concoctions to make business go well. Snakes and men, they were part of your fear in the land of your birth.

In the forests, you feared lone men you saw in the scanty forests where you herded cattle and sang praises to the birds which you killed with the power of your catapult and arrow. If the arrows did not work, you put gum on the sticks and trapped the birds. You put long sticks covered with gum where the birds came in search of grain or water. Then you hid a short distance away, hearts throbbing, eyes wide open, stomachs growling, concealed from the eyes of the birds of the sky. You hid there until weavers or other birds swarmed into your traps. Then they perched on the gum-pasted sticks and you ran, your blood boiling, to strangle them, break their beaks, hit them with sticks, your mouth already watering as you saw mangled feathers and blood.

Sometimes you were lucky enough to get the go-away-bird himself, the big chief of the tall trees. He needed a thick layer of gum and a heavy stick so he could not fly away with the traps. If you got the go-away-bird himself, maybe you could get a small piece of the bird from your father to encourage your warrior's ways. Sons of Lazarus, your father once overheard your bitter anger. He was eating the go-away-bird and not looking back. The trapper of birds had nothing to do with how they were eaten.

It brought much pride to come home with a bundle of birds stuck in the woven-fibre bags which you so proudly carried with you into the forests. If you caught big birds, you dangled them loosely on a shoulder string. Everybody saw that in you was a hunter, a warrior of many years to come. All the eyes of the village gazed in admiration. And you feared that it might be one more reason why witches would agree to invade your sleeping mat the same night, taking you for their horse for the night, leaving their hyenas to rest for a while. That is if they were kind.

The girls' eyes also went with you to the forests and back. They ran to you, taking you captive so they could see what was inside your bags. 'Come, show us what you caught,' they shouted at you, in voices that were gently provocative. You felt shy and small in front of them. A little fear too because you did not know what they wanted to do with you.

Girls, sometimes they did all sorts of things with you. They pulled down your pants and made you feel ashamed. They named all you had inside those pants and you cried as if you had been hurt by things worse than words. 'Oh, our mother, did you make us women for this?' they shouted, examining you, a trapped animal.

You only cried and looked, their firm hands holding you tight so they could see what they wanted to see without any hurry.

'What will you give me if I show you?' you wanted to know.

'This,' they said, exposing their small breasts for you to come and fondle at will if you gave them what you had trapped. They would secretly roast the small bird without drawing the attention of their mothers. You felt a man after touching the breast of the little girl. A man, happy to provide for the woman you had chosen.

At the *mahumbwe* games, you fondled the breasts of the girl who had taken a small bird from you. She was your wife. You stood up and became a father, ordering her to bring some water, father is thirsty, bring some food, father is hungry. Don't let the children play with my carvings, I am going to the forest to cut poles to build another cattle pen.

In the glare of the new moon, you danced with the familiar girls. You danced with them, feeling a certain weight inside you, dancing all the time, not minding the dust which your feet cast into the night air. You kicked the air and breathed the dust in which your umbilical cord had been buried. You heard too the old songs of the owls and knew the owners of those night birds.

On your way home, you knew whose ghosts inhabited which anthill. So you had to be careful not to insult the relatives of the owners of those ghosts hiding where you knew. The rivers, the hills, the streams and the anthills, they were the hiding places of the ghosts which caused you sleepless nights. It did not matter, though. They were familiar ghosts and ogres. They played tricks on you and you played tricks with them. Life had to go on.

But this new land which your father dreamt about had sounded different and far away like those stories that come to you in a dream. It had been a dream. The stories he had told you were of man and wild animal sitting together for a meal without a quarrel. He had sat you by the fireside, on a dark night, at the place where only men and boys sat to recount the year's signs and listen to the stories of life and death . . .

'Once upon a time, Hare and Baboon went to look for girls. In the place of their birth, there were not many pretty girls. Hare had heard of distant lands where they could go and find the most beautiful girls in the whole land, the whole earth. The girls there were so pretty that if you looked at them during the day their beauty blinded your eyes. Their feet, smiling faces, erect breasts, so supple.

'Then one day something in Hare's breast said he should see the girls from far-away places. His heart was restless. He could not go alone. It was far away and some other wild animal might see him walking alone along the footpath and think it was not a bad idea to clean their mouth with this small piece of meat. Hare could not imagine that happening to him. He needed someone to walk with so the distance could be killed with talk and song.

'Hare had a sweet tongue. He could ask you to sell him your tail and you would happily do it without asking any questions. He moved his long ears this way and that as if to give you fresh air. He is kind, you would feel. Then: can you accompany me to the land of the prettiest girls, the most charming, most endearing, with the sweetest voices you have ever heard? The girls in those lands are so forthcoming. They will not forbid you to sleep with them even in the open plains, in the valleys, under the trees. Their parents do not care. They know that a beautiful gourd must contain water some day.

'Baboon was one man who did not want to be left out of such happenings. As soon as Hare had finished part of his story, Baboon was already wagging his stiff tail, smearing it with oil so the girls would be attracted to him before they got carried away with Hare's large ears. He even powdered the dark hairs of his face to make them into a rich, shiny dark.

'As they walked along, Baboon and Hare, friends since the beginning of time, felt they were getting hungry. They needed some food. Baboon's stomach was already growling. You could hear it from distant hills, as if a lion was growling from a cave.

'Hare, the fast runner that he is, asked Baboon to remain behind for a while. "Sit on some tree branch to watch if there are movements in the nearby thickets." And Hare ran off.

'On his return, Hare brought a gourd full of frothy milk, well milked by Hare's own clean hands. Baboon's mouth was already watering as soon as he saw the overflowing gourd of milk. "I think we must remain in this place for a while. All this milk. If the people of this land have such milk in their cows, they must also have pretty daughters from their wombs," Baboon was quick to suggest.

'Oh, was the milk good, frothing as it went down the mouth of the hungry Baboon. His hands, dark and dirty because he walked carelessly along the footpath with brown soil, were white with the milk from the gourd.

' "I thought you were the only one who fell for temptation," Hare mumbled in the midst of gulpfuls of milk. "I too think we should remain here for a while. The land of pretty girls is still many forests away. We will have more milk and then continue on our journey." Hare was quick to admit his own weakness for this milk, as fresh and warm as if it had just come from the udder of a cow. Hare could not remember any moment in his life when he had stolen such rich milk from the owners of the cows. He had stolen some milk which tasted like water. Bad farmers, he had cursed, they must be fed to the hungry lion who makes noise in the forest every day, calling himself King of the Forest.

' "I hear you well," Baboon agreed with his friend.

' "But Uncle Baboon, this time you will have to go yourself. I can't be the one to show you the land of pretty girls, the land of frothy milk, everything. I cannot be the one to do all that for you. I know we are close relatives, but to think that I have to run around for you all the time—this is a bit too much," Hare complained. He knew that in their friendship he had cheated Baboon so many times that both had lost count.

' "That is no problem, my dear Hare. You know the tricks. Teach me and it will be done perfectly. What can I not do for this milk? So tasty and frothy, it makes me feel like changing my home to come and live here." Baboon was all enthusiasm, his heart beating fast.

' "I know all the tricks. You carry this calabash with you, hanging it loosely in this net. When you go into the cattle pen, you quietly milk the cows, the fat ones. You milk until the calabash is full. If the cows ask you what you are doing, tell them you are the new herd boy. Tell them you milk them early in order to impress your masters. Tell them any cow which does not give you all its milk will be slaughtered during the celebrations for the new harvest." Hare cleared his throat.

' "I see." Baboon saw the plan clearly. "It looks well to me." Already Baboon could see himself creeping quietly into the cattle pen in the middle of the night, calabash in hand, pulling the teats of the udders of the cows, feeling the warmth of the milk in his palms, soothed by it all. The owners of the cows could snore, and no one would be bothered, Baboon thought.

' "Then, the difficult part. On your way back, it might be light already. The place is far away. You will meet people with inquisitive eyes and noses. The first thing they will always do is to greet you and ask you where you are coming from and where you are going. Tell them you had gone to visit a relative who has an unknown disease, and that you also found out that his crops were attacked by large swarms of brown locusts. So, since you do not hate well-fried brown locusts, you picked some and they are in your bag right now. If anyone wants to see them, tell them they are still alive and might fly away. But inside your heart you know that they are not locusts but fresh milk frothing for us to drink." Hare was through with his tricks of theft.

'Baboon, meanwhile, nodded and smiled, his tail wagging clumsily.

'The following morning, Baboon came back crying, with neither milk nor calabash.

'"What happened?" Hare wanted to know.

'"I met some people on my way back. They asked me what I was carrying and I told them I was carrying brown locusts but inside my heart I knew I was carrying fresh milk frothing for me and Hare to drink soon." Baboon went on sobbing as Hare laughed and wished he had gone himself.

'"No, Uncle Baboon, you were not supposed to tell them what was inside your heart." Hare laughed, walking along the footpath, a cloud of angry dust shooting into the air. The journey to the land of pretty girls had started. The land where only pretty girls were allowed to live. All others were killed soon after birth.

'"You know what?" Baboon said as they walked along.

'"What?" Hare was taken aback.

'"The milk today was rotten," Baboon said, his eyes still moist with tears.

'"I know," Hare replied.'

The land of far-away tales of animals will soon be ours, you say, as stories of vultures and men sharing the carcasses of dead animals in the wild overwhelm you like soot dropping from a roof. Elephants with rumbling stomachs, roaring lions, greedy hyenas and jackals, every animal that is mentioned in the folktales, they will be there for all to see, free as the morning wind. Tales of the night make you breathless, thinking: What a world! People and animals, sharing the land together, singing together, dying together.

Years later, a new homestead already stands by the holy hill, the huts standing like soldiers at attention. New fireplaces, new roofs, with a smell you do not have words for. New lands, smelling fresh like green grass squeezed between the palms of the hand, are opened by the felling of giant trees whose shadows run from one anthill to another invisible anthill. The new soil, turning unwillingly, smells so different from anything that has ever touched your nostrils.

Is this the land of animals on the hills and in the rivers, going about their ways without much fear of you or anyone who wanders by? Touch the soil, your heart says. Touch it. Breathe it. Feel its rich coarseness, rebellious.

The birds, too, circle the sky like tiny clouds drifting to nowhere in particular, their feathers firm and unruffled. A string of long-necked vultures cross the sky to the carcass of some wild animal killed by marauding hunters.

You feel you are next in the line of those to be visited by the ghostly birds. The songs of the other little birds confuse you. So gentle and welcoming to your lost heart. But there is pain still inside you. You don't know the words of the language of those little birds. No one has been kind enough to tell you their names. They are simply birds. Birds with long beaks, birds with colourful necks, birds with shiny black feathers. Birds. Birds. How do you answer back to their calls when you don't understand their words? You go to sleep without knowing which bird sings the earliest song for you to wake up. Morning will come in a flood of so many voices you do not understand. It is as if every night is your last breath.

In this land of Gotami, the playground is empty. No children play there. The songs that brought you up are silent. The children are afraid of the moon. Bathed in the moonlight, they can see far away into the night. But they know wild animals can also see them from far away, or from nearby in the tall grass where they are hiding, waiting for their chance to kill. You are afraid.

At night warthogs come and take their share of your father's crops.

Baboons and monkeys too, the ones not to be insulted, climb the trees and jump across the empty sky above your heads. They sing different songs from the ones that you heard when you were growing up.

Insects, cicadas, sing shriekier songs of the pain of sharing the flowers with sheep and goats, the new arrivals. Startled birds sing warning songs that seem to say: We hate you for coming! New death, go away!

Here, everything is different. The sun comes out from the wrong sky. The rivers flow upstream. The fingers of the hills point in the wrong direction, away from where you were born, as if to point to your death. When you sing or shout to the donkeys and the cattle, the echoes come back muffled and sinister. Angry echoes of Gotami's people's voice. You are afraid of the night, and the day too, flooding your heart with so many worries every day.

You are afraid of yourself. It is a deep fear of not knowing yourself. A fear so deep it makes you silent like one waiting for a never-arriving visitor. All the faces around you tell you of their deep fear which no one seems able to give words to. There are no names here. No one has a name for anything. No one knows the shape of the night. No one dreams of the shape of the day to come. Darkness. All the darkness of the world is here. No witches, since the wild beasts would eat them. Only dreams of far-away places, far from this place of your father's dreams.

Gotami's lands, you hear yourself say, they are wild and full of fear, unknowable dreams.

When your mothers plant seeds in Gotami's soil, the fields are green before you know it. It is like a miracle. Rich, fertile soil gives life to a new crop in abundance. Maize. Cotton. The other crops which you saw in the land of your birth are now mere stories.

Your father stands on the edge of the field, on a hot moist day, listening to the voices of the maize plants talking. He touches the leaves of the plants and mumbles words about this life measured in maize cobs. From each leaf he can feel the pulse of the plant. The leaves shush to him, soothing his heart, whispering to him the stories of wealth and plenty which he has told everyone for so long. I wish everyone back home could see this, he thinks aloud, the plants overhearing the yearnings of his flying soul. Alone, he walks the fields, talking to the soil, hearing messages from the plants, asking some plants why they should be thin when all the others are fat. The man touches the soil in his hands and with the soles of his bare feet. An outburst of joy overpowers him like a man in a trance. All the time he whistles a nameless tune, his passion afloat. The greenness seems to be his own greenness, fresh and juicy.

In these moments, he forgets about you all, about everything, about the graves of his ancestors abandoned in far-away lands. He is alone, the man who dreams alone without the interference of the dead and the living. Alone with these hills and rivers which talk to him in a language only he can understand. Alone with the select few whom only he can see and share songs with. Alone with voices from the new lands, from the leaves of the crops, the ripples of the waters of the new rivers, the stars spread mysteriously on this new sky which seems so far from everything.

Did you watch your father walk among the cattle and the sheep? No, not the goats. They don't please him. Personality. They don't have personality. He hates them for that. He would rather leave the goat business to the women, his wives. Your father would listen to the cattle breathing, their sharp teeth mowing the tall grass, grazing. He sits down to see them, his eyes flaming. His heart too. Thanks to the ancestors for having given me this wealth. He touches them and calls each by its name. Every one of them born today or yesterday has a name already. He knows them. They are his new children. Whenever he calls them, they raise their heads to say, yes, we can hear you, master.

Star was the name of the bull with a dot on its forehead. A bull bought from the greedy white farmer. MaMhlanga was the name of the cow which gave more milk than all the others. MaDube, this rebellious cow which refuses to allow anyone to touch her udders. The one which overturns the milk jar. He hears their breath and feels their hearts, ailing or healthy. On their faces he sees health or disease before the LDO can tell him. For hours, for days, years, he stands by a bull or a cow, stroking its nose, touching its back, imagining how happy the animal is in these seas of green pastures. Grass and leaves, all green, hanging loosely on the face of the earth.

Your father talks with the calves too, as if to ask them what they want to be when they grow up. Milk, do you like your new milk? What is it like, jumping up in the sky, in this heaven of grass and leaves? he asks them.

The cows, bulls and calves lick his fingers and palms, nodding their heads with joy.

And when the plough turns the soil, your father is there, standing firm, his hands smeared with the soil he picked up to satisfy his heart. Isn't that what the LDO always did? His eyes tell him the goodness or badness of the lump of black soil in his hands. This land gives me what I want, he says, his voice swallowed by the rattling of the tractor. Yields of grain, cotton, birds jumping from tree to tree in song and dance, wild animals, rains which know no seasons. Rivers bursting with fish and croaking frogs any time of the year.

At harvest time, no one eats from the fields before the rituals of offering the new crops to the ancestors are performed. Your father holds the large mealie cobs and tells the ancestors that it is not his hands holding the cobs but theirs. It is their voices which commanded the crops to grow. He prays for better harvests every year and gets them. He prays for no deaths in the family and his prayers are answered, since there is no grave yet near the new homestead. For many years you grow up thinking that death is for other people, not you and your sisters and brothers. Death is far away from you. Graves are distant things: you only hear about it in folktales. They are like distant clouds in the dry season.

'This land,' you hear your father's voice say. 'The graves of my fathers, if only they were here,' he says only rarely, when his heart is in discomfort, at night.

It is day. The sky is open. You can see little rivers up in the sky, formed by patterns of big and small clouds. A man sees a firefly, in broad daylight. He follows it, his heart feverish. He follows it, walking in a hurry like one about to catch the little fire of the fly. The man stops, walks again, touches a leaf and sighs. He has missed the glow of the firefly in his hands. He bends, then kneels to touch the green plants that are his life. The plants and the firefly merge into one large flame of joy. He touches the soil and praises it for keeping both the firefly and the plants. If he smells it, he will feel his heart exploding with a new laughter. The palms of the man tell him so. He is not alone any more. The plants, the fireflies, the birds perching on his head, all the life around him, all the friends. Life. Old friends. New friends to be born with the coming of another season.

A leaf drops in front of me, yellow, dying. A letter falling from the dark-blue sky full of rivers of water and dew. Woven patterns like the palm of a child appear on the leaf. A greeting from the dead. Soft whispers of the winds in my ears. Another leaf, yellow like a flower, falls with a *shshshs*, hissing like a friend, soft. Another leaf follows the stream of leaves, a feather floating in the wind. Feather and firefly merge into one big flame of joy. It sings a little tickling tune of its escape, insulting me for interfering.

A little bird is startled and rushes out of my way, its wings flapping in the dry grass as if it wanted to weave a mat of grass and feathers. Little birds like this one bring laughter to my heart. You kill it with a catapult, all you have is a small pile of feathers. You can't see the little bird after throwing it into the fire to roast. Silence. Hey, even lizards dance when I pass by. Lizards. Lizards. *Dhambakura rovera musoro pasi, mai vanogwara kumba. Dhambakura rovera musoro pasi, mai vanogwara kumba.* Songs of youth. Children and lizards playing together.

They are the same age, children and lizards. So fond of each other.

People are deaf, though. They sit on their ears when I talk. Words irritate their ears. But words which have been spoken enter the ear and spread their mat there. When I say death is afraid of me, people think I am not serious. When the sun shines and the wind blows gently in the face, it is only a fool who dies. I have worked hard for all this. Children, wives, granaries full of grain. Sheds. Machines that roar in a way my ancestors never imagined. It is mine. From hands that work. Wealth comes from hands that work and feet that walk. Buttocks never brought anyone anything.

I know I am alone, sweating in these lands, far away from the voices which would have praised me. Far away from familiar clouds whose movements and colours I know how to read. But here I own what I own. The soil. The sky above my lands. The moon glowing up there in the night. This soil, which you stand on, is mine. The grass, the snakes, the ants. Even the marauding hyenas. They are mine. I can order them to die or live. I give life to and take life away from those animals I see fit to die or live. *Basopo lo inja.* Danger, *skelemu*. I saw it written on the gates to the houses of white men many years ago. My days as a milk-delivery boy. A man who owns a spear makes rules about how it must be used.

Cattle, goats, lambs, birds, fireflies, the very river which flows through my farm. I own them all. I will die when all this is finished. For now, let me see and feel my heart settle in my breast. I will forget the days when I woke up to lick the dirty shoes of the white man. Those were the days! Yes, baas. I am selling eggs, baas. Sorry about selling eggs to you, baas. But my chickens are good. They don't eat what should not be eaten by good chickens. Oh, whatever price you can offer me, baas. I will feed my children. Baas! Baas! At the same time baas plays with his dog. Nothing disturbs him. I remember the white man who took all the eggs from my basket and gave me a cup of tea in an old grease can. I drank the tea, bowed my thanks and went away to vomit. I said to myself, when will this end? Does it end through friendship with the white man or through hating him? If I befriend him, maybe he will one day tell me the tricks of his fathers, I said to myself.

So, time came and I took the hoe and the plough. I delivered ripe watermelons, pumpkins, sugarcane, peanuts and groundnuts to Indians in the city. Indians who took what you grew in your own garden and sold it back to you to enrich themselves. *Buya tinapangana*, they always shouted at me, asking me to give them the product of my sweat, free. I made the little money I could make out of them. Two shillings for a bag of good peanuts. Two pence for a watermelon. Three pence for a laying chicken.

LDO, tell me, what can my hands not do which your people have done to enrich themselves?

Belly of the purse, he says. Belly of the purse.

Remember the day the LDO came to crown me Master Farmer? All the eyes of the village were on me. Eyes of the witches. Eyes of the diviners and medicine-men.

Envious eyes of greed and admiration. A dream takes shape. A night of no sleep brings many nights of better sleep. A nestling which hesitates to fly will never fly.

Life was like that. I was life and it was me. I learnt that life had to change. Look at the soil and ask it what you want, I told myself. Soil, is it you from whom the white man takes wealth? Sweat. Hands and feet. My children must go to school, girls and boys. Sweat some more to feed the mouths which open like mouths of nestlings in your sleep.

'Girls to school?' My friend Tsapi laughed at me. 'You must have been converted by the preachers from the church. How can a man like you send girls to school? Can't you see I send only boys to school? If you want to be told from a mouth which does not hide issues, send a girl to school and you are sending back the money to the in-laws where you paid the bride-price to bring a woman into your house. You are burning money like firewood, with your eyes wide open. Girls must only go to school to enable them to read letters from their suitors. Nothing more.' Tsapi was adamant. He warned me, his tyre sandals gripping the sand of the footpath as we walked to his home.

Tsapi had asked his 'boys' to slaughter a small cow for us. To eat while we talked about the burdens of our hearts. It was his habit to shed a little blood, a little life, so his friends could eat and throw away the cares of the world. A rich man must once in a while call his friends to eat, celebrating the kindness of life. Ancestors will also

be happy that way. Such moments need not be inter-
rupted by men who talk like women, Tsapi would say.

'If girls don't go to school, Tsapi, where will we get
nurses and schoolmistresses?' I threw the bait at him,
rather carelessly. Clever thoughts sometimes come after
foolish questions.

'Ah, ah! Ah, ah! Who told you that the nurse should
come from your own house? Did the nurses tell you what
was in their houses? Maybe they do not have fathers.'
His mouth was quick.

I see his point as he talks, but worries harass me. My
girls. The girls who will bring cattle into my home. I try
to persuade myself that I will follow Tsapi's advice even
if I do not entirely agree with him. His words might bear
fruit later in life, I think. The man laughs at foolishness
whenever he sees it. The hoarse voice can itch your blood.
Tsapi had laughed so loud his wives came outside their
huts to see if the man had choked from a piece of meat.

Foolishness. Girls to school. No. I see the point more
clearly now. None of my girls went to school long enough
to be nurses and teachers. They can read the letters of
their lovers. That is all. Who said one must drink the
whole well in order to quench one's thirst? A small
calabash of water will do sometimes. Those girls can
now go to night school with their husbands. Would they
have worked in the fields had I sent them to school in my
foolishness? No. All they would be doing now is brush
their teeth, bathe, eat and sleep, with the skin of their
palms as soft as cotton wool.

You see this soil, this bird which flew past me, this green crop whispering into my ears? I did not go to school myself. All I did was to work hard. Sweat.

The other day the LDO, a young white man, called me 'mister'. Not many Africans have ever been called 'mister' by a white man. Old man or young man, they call you 'my boy'. I know they think we are animals, wild all the time. Sometimes they are right. The Boers were harsh to us in the mines. Harsh like hot pepper. A kick on the buttocks. A blow on the nose. Insults. Our people do not want to work. They work a little bit, look at the sun, put away the hoe or the plough, and look for somewhere to dance and sing. The white man wants to see us work, not sit and idle around like small children. Buttocks never brought anyone any wealth. Feet and hands bring wealth. Wipe away sweat. Sing and dance later when the work has been done. Do not wake up in the morning, looking for a beer party, preparing songs and dances for celebration. Follow the footpath to where the sound of the drum is coming from. Drums are made of wood and the skin of strong oxen. If you are lazy, how do you get the strong oxen? No, the white man is right. I worked for him and learnt that life begins and ends with hard work. I am now somebody because hard work gave me new strength.

To die now would be to ask the sun to set at midday. Illness can be cured. Death is unnecessary when a flower is blooming. Now I can walk and the soles of my feet rest on the warm soil of my land. Those who smiled at my death will wear wilted faces again. This soil, my soul, so gentle and soothing, tickling my bare soles, the maize whispering to me songs of a new communion with the land.

The birds, too, sing their songs of faith in me. In the streams I will bathe away the darkness of my life. The sky opens. I see through it and breathe again that sigh of relief which many people hate to see on my face.

The morning comes in whispers the following day. The red sky is harsh. There are whispers in the air. And shouts too. The sun looks an angry red. Your father lies under the early-morning shade of the *musuma* tree. He breathes rather faintly. When people ask him how the night was with him, he stares at them. The body is healthy, but the mind roams to far-away places. In these days of shameless witches and pretentious medicine-men, it is not possible to sleep in peace. Your father silently thinks: The crow ate and rubbed its beak in the dust. I am afraid. A voice startles me out of my nightly reveries. Should I run after the cattle, my heart pounding with this new fear of a trap within me? Let me break through the mesh of leaves and creepers that entangles my legs, my soul. Break them apart. Tear them to pieces. Fly. Escape from the spider's web. The cattle! The cattle! The wealth is flowing down the flooded river. Will someone not help? Help, someone! There is a scar deep on the cloud high up in the sky. Far away.

Part 2

Women

1966 – Play

YOU HEAR CHILDREN'S voices, far away, the waves of sounds getting nearer, the wind wafting them to your ears, your heart, like a perfume from the wild flowers with wild wings which fly in the air, scattering the yellow powder so generously into the air you breathe. You try to sleep. Mother has said so. You must sleep. Yesterday you came back from the arena of the moonlight, crying, hurt by the insults from the careless lips of the other children. But still your heart wants to disobey your mother's stern voice.

Your heart pounds on the side of your ribs, small bones inside you which you feel vibrating with the rhythms of the big voices of the children of your age. They are playing in the bewitching playground of the new moonlight. The handclaps, the rhythmic stamping of young feet, it all reaches your ears and knocks on the door of your heart. The doors of your yearning.

Yelling voices tell you that even the voice of death can be disobeyed in these things. Still, the moon bewitches you with its flood of light, telling you to sing and dance with the other children.

'Devil,' you name your mother in a whisper no one can hear. She has been transformed into a monster. A devil who should have stayed in the home of her own parents. She should not have dared come to your father's home to steal the moon from you. All those songs spilling into the night without you nearby!

The voices of the other children mingle so freely with the moonlight, the night, the sleep you hate to have. The songs of the children continue to drift from songs of childish courtship to songs insulting the lazy, good-for-nothings of the village. There are songs of graceful dance and movement too. You listen and your heart aches as if it would burst and let you die. A pain moves through your body like they say needles do if they enter your blood, stinging here, pinching there, jerking there, everywhere. You feel the *hurukuru* powder has been smeared by a cruel person on your skin. It is sore. You listen carefully as the children go into the game of naming everyone from the same mother in the correct order of their birth. That is the game at which you beat all of those voices you can hear out in the moonlight. But you are not there. If only you were there! If only you were there! After all, if you are not there, the children will not name you. You are like a child who died many years ago. The ache in your body wells up, its grip tightening on your heart as the voices waft with the wind more persuasively than before, accusing you of some form of treachery. Wake up, traitor! Wake up, traitor! Wake up, traitor! You feel the voices sail through the air, the echoes coming back to you from your own heart, which has become a dark cave.

Soloist:	*Dudu muduri.*
Others:	*Kache!*

Soloist:	*Dudu muduri.*
Others:	*Kache!*

Soloist:	*Raviro muduri.*
Others:	*Kache!*

Soloist:	*Chipo muduri.*
Others:	*Kache!*

Soloist:	*Rambai muduri.*
Others:	*Kache!*

You cry softly, your tears hidden under the blankets. Mother hears the sniffing of your tearful nose under the old blanket. She is enraged. She stops her own singing about her own problems which you don't care about for now. She knocks the plates around in her anger. Maybe they will break. That way she will learn her lesson, you think.

The fire is almost dead now in the old fireplace which brought you up. She does not put on more firewood. It is hard to walk all that distance to the hills to fetch some more firewood. In her rage, she throws away the blanket that covers you, threatening to hurt you with the slap of her palm which has just cooked for you. She will break your skull one of these days. Foolish boy, with a head full of worms and useless lizards, she curses.

'Go and play! But do not sleep there!' you hear her order. Still you think she does not mean it. You wait a little longer to see if she will persuade you to go. 'I said you can go and play with the others. Bring back all the dust of the soil with you,' your mother says, mocking you for always coming back almost buried in the dust of the dance arena. She is angry, but for now she is resigned to it.

You jump out of the hut, your heart free like the heart of a little bird released from the hands of a hungry person, the hands of death by plucking and roasting. You fly and fly and fly until you perch at the arena where the others have been wondering where you have been the whole night. 'In your mother's skirts,' they say scornfully. You simply ignore them and listen to the sound of the flow of the feelings, the flow of music and the dance. And before anyone can invite you, the dance is already in your blood, spilling. You breathe it. You smell it. You touch it in the air, and the flame of dance swallows you until you forget that your pants are torn in shameful places.

Once you are in the arena, the moonshine becomes more intoxicating. You see all these children from your father's homestead. There are no children from the neighbours. Only children of the same blood. The songs you have left in far-away places are born again in the voices of children of your own mothers. Many mothers, young and old. Young brothers and sisters, elder brothers and sisters, all bathing in the joys of the moon and the dances of the places they now only remember.

With your breath fading, you recite the names of all the children, then play the games of naming the trees, the rivers, the hills and mountains. You can only name the rivers and hills of the place where you were born.

The names of the children from your different mothers, all of them, in their correct order of birth. Some have since vanished into the mysterious world of work in faraway places, far away in the mines, never to return. You still name them. They are not dead.

In your game of naming, you name the children from one mother to the rhythm of hand clapping and soft stamping of feet. If a reciter stammers or stops to remember, you jeer and push them out of the arena.

All the children stand in a circle. The reciter stands at the centre, clapping her hands in time to the stamping of your dancing feet. She leads the song of the game of naming. The singer must not falter. The song takes on the rhythms of pounding grain in the mortar, pounding the memory to give you all you want:

Soloist: *Dudu muduri.*
Others: *Kache!*

Soloist: *Dudu muduri.*
Others: *Kache!*

You hear the voice of the singer slicing the air, the chorus, like an eagle, capturing it in mid-air, the night swelling with names and hand claps, the barely visible dust rising on the back of the voices. You know that soon your hair will be like the white hair of a ghost. It does not matter. The names of your brothers and sisters are churned out in the dust. They touch the dust but come out clean in your memory.

When the dance grips you like a disease, you try to jump into the arena. No. Someone has already taken the centre. It does not matter. She sings the names of the children of your own mother. You think she has made a mistake. You jeer at her. Why has she not mentioned Tariro, your sister? You jeer again. Then you feel lonely. Your voice has been the only one that jeered. But you hear the singers going on as if Tariro were not part of these songs.

So, Tariro is dead. Tariro is dead, you say to yourself. She must be removed from the memories of the living. She is dead, a castaway, a reject.

Tariro, your name was not mentioned. Where is your name? Are you my sister? You ask yourself so many questions as you walk back to your mother, from whom you ran away. The dance is not over yet, but you have a pain deeper than the one you felt before when your mother would not let you go to play. You feel a sharp knife cutting through your blood, making you dizzy like someone whose itch is in a place they cannot scratch. You walk away in the invisible moonlight. The tears in your eyes make the night dark now. You are blind and deaf to everything.

Near your mother's hut, you hesitate to go in before

your tears are dry. Mother will notice and ask you if you have been in a fight already. She will whip you if you have been. She will grab you by the arm and whip you for being a weakling who cries all the time. She will be harsh with you if you are a weak child who cries when another child steps on your toe. No, it is better to hide behind the hut until your eyes are clear of tears and your face does not cry. You hide until your voice takes back its moisture of moonlight joy and laughter. In the silence of the night, you hear your small heart throbbing, and you worry that your mother will hear it from inside the hut.

'Who is that?' mother asks. She is already outside the hut. You move backwards to try to evade her searching eyes in the moonlight. Your feet made a sound when you moved. She heard it. 'Who is that hiding?' she wonders.

'It's me,' you say, trying hard to make your voice normal.

'Me who?' She is agitated.

'Me, Mucha,' you feebly answer back, trying to force joy into your voice to make her think you were playing hide-and-seek with her in the semi-darkness.

'Yes, me, crying, already back! So it was only your itching buttocks which were saying don't sit, don't sit. And you come back, crying to me? With a wound somewhere so I can start nursing wounds again. Blood on the nose every night. What happened?' You feel her anger spilling into the air, like a warm fire heating the area around the fireplace.

'We were singing *Dudu muduri*. They refused to name Tariro. They say she should not be mentioned.' Tears start flowing again, drowning your face. Tears tears tears. Sobs. Pain in your chest. A stream of pain inside your whole body. Your mother takes you into her arms like a little baby. She sits you down by the fire before laying you down to sleep under your old blankets. She rekindles the dying fire. Soon you hear the cry of her grinding stone. She bursts out in song, saying things you do not understand. Painful things about her sore heart, her people, everything, singing into the night until you hear her voice weaving in and out of your dreams of Tariro. Am I not a child that you give me so much pain? Was I not born that you give me so much pain? Happiness you give to those who were born well. For me, I see happiness only in dreams.

You cry in the dream when a woman shows you where Tariro, your sister, is. She is silent as she shows you the bare grave. No, you cannot ask anyone about her death. People here speak a strange language. See and walk away like a shadow. This is food for the eyes only, the tongue may rest . . .

1958 – Tariro

It had been early in the morning, the hour before the lazy ones and the not-so-lazy could wake up to go to the fields, the hour when elephants went to bathe and the little jackals and other small animals followed them in the hope that they would find themselves as large as the elephants if they bathed where the elephants bathed their hills of bodies. We want to see what herbs they smear on their bodies in this early hour, a jackal said. All the other tiny animals whispered their consent. But the elephants ignored the thin voices. They trudged along to the river, to bathe in the white sand and the muddy water of the river. It was these tiny animals which must be pitied, the elephants thought.

That was the hour when a man arrived at your father's homestead, wielding a walking stick, a knobkerrie, and words in his mouth. His skin aprons were shiny with new oil that he had asked his wife to smear on them the night before. 'Is anything up?' she had wondered. The man had ignored her, asking her to do as she was told.

It appeared the man had large words in his mind. He simply sat there and scratched his beard, waiting for the father of the homestead to wake up.

Waking up had always been the easiest thing on earth for your father. A single blink of the eye, no yawning, and the man was out of the house in a moment. There had been sounds of footsteps outside. He heard them and wondered who it could be so early in the day. Footsteps, you never know what they bring, he said to his young wife, leaving her warm body in the blankets. It was footsteps which had brought messages of death in life. It was footsteps which had brought invitations to a beer drink.

Footsteps had carried news of an impending war. When the white man came into our lands, it was footsteps that brought him. Even those that flew high up in the sky in flying machines, they landed and walked to deliver whatever it was that they carried. Only footsteps could go far and bring news. Discoveries are made by feet, not by buttocks, the ancestors had said long before anyone was born. Footsteps. Walk and you will prosper. Sit on your buttocks and you will remain poor the rest of your life. Buttocks are the friends of poverty, your father thought. Whenever a man was lazy, he was soon nicknamed The-One-Who-Trusts-His-Buttocks. A shameful name. But the village soon learnt to call him that way without feeling ashamed. Even children would call him that in broad daylight if they got the opportunity. The-One-Who-Trusts-His-Buttocks is coming, they sang whenever they saw the man passing by, impotently furious. He could not afford to beat the children. You do not beat up children for shouting your nickname. It was an unheard-of sacrilege. And if you beat them for that, the name stuck on you like a tick. Why did the father of so-and-so punish the children? voices would ask all over the village. The question went round and round like the rope swing on which the village children swung around until their heads were dizzy. Round and round and round and round. The answers too would go round and round, like an echo caught between two neighbouring hills. Soon, the name caught on to the man. Every village used it whichever way they wanted . . .

He-Who-Sits-on-His-Buttocks, are you childless?
He-Who-Sits-on-His-Buttocks, you beat children.
He-Who-Sits-on-His-Buttocks all day

Did the children give you another name?
Come, onlookers of this village,
See him of angry buttocks.
He has a wife,
All sitting on his buttocks.

Farmers of this land,
He-of-Angry-Buttocks needs a basket.
He needs a basket full of grain.
Give him alms, the poor man.
He sits from sunrise to sunset,
Following the shadows, on his stool.

Onlookers of the village,
Watch out and guard your daughters.
Buttocks also wants to marry a new wife.
Look at the back of his loincloth,
Patched at the back,
Like a baboon's behind.

Songs and riddles spread in the heads of the villagers
for a man who refused a nickname. Children, young
maidens, men at the beer drink, everybody. Some said
even the cockerels of the village had begun to shout:
Have you seen buttocks that *siiiiit*? Have you seen
buttocks that *siiiit*? Until the birds of the forests answered
back: Which ones? The ones that wear out the hardest
skin-cloth? Which ones? The ones that wear out the
hardest skin-cloth?

At night children gathered to play games of riddles

with anything they could imagine. Riddles brightened the dark night for them.

Tapiwa: That which beat itself and cried?
Nyarai: A cockerel which beats its wings before crying.

Tapiwa: That which sings and people close their nostrils?
Nyarai: A person passing bad air. (Laughter.)

Nyarai: A person whose skin-cloth is worn at the back?
Tapiwa: Mafukidze, the village loiterer.

And so the night went on. Let the children play. Without play, what will they be? The elders curse the angry man.

The sky was still a queer mixture of blue and red and yellow when the man arrived. His heart seemed to be carrying heavy matters.

Your father woke up, coughed dryly and walked out as soon as he had heard the man announce his arrival insistently, waiting for a hurried answer. A hoarse, half-awake voice had responded from within the house, authorizing the man to enter the homestead. The stranger had not heard the voice and continued. The voice went on until the stranger had heard it and so calmed down, imagining the owner of the voice wearing his tyre sandals or having the last few words of the night with his wife.

'Oh, it is you, Mafunga! Has the earth woken on the wrong side that your feet walk in our direction so early?' your father wanted to know.

'How are you, in-law?' Mafunga inquired.

'We are peaceful. But we worry when you arrive like this, as if you were coming to announce a death,' your father went on, his pulse increasing its pace, the patterns of his sleeping mat still clearly marked on his cheeks.

'I am only a messenger, father-in-law. The carrier of guns is not the one who fires them,' retorted Mafunga.

'I know that the messenger does not deserve to be seen with scars. I hope you do not have weighty words which will need serious men around me,' your father said.

'Oh, no!' the messenger was quick to point out, a hesitant smile flashing on his face. 'It is just words, serious and not so serious. I bring greetings from the man who plays drums. He says the story of the girl, I mean the tall one, Tariro, is a good story. He accepts the offer as it should be accepted in the old ways of our ancestors. He only thinks the girl might be too young for him, since he is a man whose destination is nearer than where he started from. That is his only worry. It will mean the young woman will sooner know widowhood than marriage,' Mafunga went on.

'Ah, Mafunga, you talk like a child. Doesn't Musindo, at his age, know that a man who marries a young wife also marries for those of his blood who are not yet born?' Your father smiled, his heart sensing a man with a good mission.

As Mafunga walks away when the sun's rays are already above the tall trees, a daughter has a husband. She does not know the whole story. She sleeps and wakes up to go to the well with the other girls. She sings songs which cry the yearnings of her heart, for the day she will be courted by the most handsome boy of the village, worshipping her like a goddess, saying all the beautiful things about her long neck, the style of her walking, the gap in her teeth. She sings and dances at the well when she sees her face for the first time in the water of the well:

'Ah, hinga ndakanaka!
Ah, hinga ndakanaka!
Ah, hinga ndakanaka!'

'Oh, how beautiful I am!
Oh, how beautiful I am!
Oh, how beautiful I am!'

The girl swaggers home, twisting her waist, balancing the gourd on her head in the style of women whom she has seen carrying waterpots with such grace, their necks erect like giraffes', their movement smooth as the flight of an eagle. Woman with the neck of a gazelle, wait for me before I kill myself. Woman whose steps are like one grinding on the stone, tell your mother a man is bewitched by your beauty. Woman with a gap in your front teeth, tell your brother he will see my footprints every day in your homestead. Woman who eats only milk for fear of dirtying your teeth, you have destroyed my heart. Beautiful maiden, tell your father to build a bigger cattle pen soon.

Tariro kneels at the door of the hut to unload her

gourd, singing inside her heart the joys and sorrows of motherhood she can see clearly ahead of her.

As for school, it can wait until her own children go to waste their time with the angry schoolteacher. The one who is said to tell people about places he has never seen as if he had been there himself. Tariro has seen girls whose girlhood was wasted at the school. Big girls listening to children's stories told badly by the teacher. No man wanted to marry them. Their breasts were flat and drab like rotten fruit, as if they had suckled several children already. 'Grandmothers' they were called by the young men in search of young maidens to bring a new fire to their homestead, a new warmth. 'Wives of the teacher,' the mocking voices had said in her ears, in her sleep. Didn't the village drunks sing about the teachers? 'Teachers, you cry for lack of women, don't you have eyes to see? What do you cry for, teachers? The women are right under your noses. Can't you see the schoolgirls, breasts erect like the horns of a small bull? Can't you see the schoolgirls, with eyes like full moons? Teachers, open your eyes. See the schoolgirls with faces, showing not even a rumour of wrinkles.' The night voices had sung, in her ears and in the hearts of the whole village.

Some teachers heard the songs, swallowed the bait, and no one ever heard about their teaching again till death. Others heard it and heard the voice of the harsh school inspector who invaded the school with a whip whenever he fancied it, beating pupil, teacher and parent in one stroke, like one possessed. When they saw schoolgirls blinding their eyes with their youthful beauty, they put eye ointment in their eyes, blaming them for bad visions.

A year later Tariro, the young girl with breasts like the small tips of a young man's thumbs, is led by two women to a place she does not know. The two women, an ageing aunt and a not-so-young 'sister', walk with her, telling her in riddles and proverbs how to take care of her man should she get married. How to cook food which does not upset the stomach of a man, how to care for the man's relatives, how to listen to the man and do as he says all the time. 'This is why you see us lasting in marriage. We were never sent back to the houses of our fathers.' They talk on and on, the echoes of their voices coming and going from the inner bowels of the dark caves of the small hills and the *dongas* of the valleys they walk past. Sometimes the two women sing, 'We have brought her, the daughter-in-law, we have brought her.' At times they stop by the footpath and pass urine without going too far into the bushes. 'No one will see us,' they say, seeing no prospect of a man coming by to shame them.

'This thing, urine, arrives without warning,' the elder woman says. 'Even at the chief's court, in the middle of serious talk, what can the chief do when it catches him except to leave the others to whisper in his absence?' she goes on as she enjoys the water passing between her ancient thighs. 'Can he send someone to go and do it for him? Not anywhere on this earth as far as I know.' The two laugh, and the hills echo their laughter.

Then they show Tariro which herbs will treat the

nhova, the sagging of the top of the head of a child. You see, if a baby cries and cries and cries, know that someone with bad medicines has crossed your footpath. Take this herb here, burn it to black ashes and smear the ashes on the top of the child's head. That is what has been done for many years, before you were born. It saves the lives of children. That is how you were saved from the mouth of death. And if your child dies because of your negligence and ignorance, you will be the laughing-stock of the whole village. They will deride you in song and dance until you run away from your husband. It is sad to see a young woman who has been sent back from her husband because she is either negligent or ignorant or lazy. Oh, the mother of the woman will not know how to live in the village. Songs and dances will be created about her in all the villages. All the people of the village will find new ways of insulting your mother. Don't be like so-and-so's mother who does not know how to bring up a daughter. Some mothers bewitch the marriages of their daughters . . .

The women talk without waiting for Tariro to answer back. She is mesmerized by this talk, which she has always heard from her own mother. Why were these two saying things to her as if her own mother had not said them so many years ago? Why would they sing this same song the whole way while they walked to an unknown place? Didn't they know a song wears itself out if people continue to sing it as if it were the last-born of all songs?

'We are going to leave you in your true home today,'

the elder woman with cracked soles says to her, suggesting some intimacy with the young girl.

'My true home? I thought we were leaving my true home behind us,' the young girl challenges the elder woman. She wonders why the two are sounding so strange, their voices so secretive.

'A woman's true people are where she is married,' the younger 'sister' tells her, her voice firm.

Tears drip from the little girl's eyes. A tear. Two. Three. Four. A flood as they arrive at Musindo's village. Colours of a swollen heart, of rains that kill everything in a flood. She sees pain and doubt, then sighs a heavy sigh like one already dying.

As soon as they see the party arriving, the women of Musindo's village erupt in song and dance in the hot afternoon. Their loincloths sway in the air, their feet drawing complicated patterns on the dusty soil. They encircle her, holding hands, twisting their waists, waving their hands in the air, dancing to a tune of marriage and child-bearing, singing on and on until the distant hills begin to sing with them. Even passers-by stop and ask, 'Whose son has married whose daughter?' before offering to perform a dance step or two of good wishes for the man of the village. May the new womb be as fertile as the earth which raises seeds and trees.

Musindo himself sits under the shade of a *musasa* tree a short distance away, happy that the offer of marriage from a man who wants to cement their friendship has finally been fulfilled, consummated like a marriage of two long-time sweethearts. It is a dream which one wakes up and finds to be true. He puffs at his pipe lazily, his ancient nostrils agreeing that it is good tobacco. The old man knows that the earth has given him happiness for all these years, and will give it to him again in his last days. Then he coughs gently, satisfied, suppressing his usual explosive, scary cough which sends children running for their lives and chickens scampering for shelter. Had the dogs not barked the other day when he was at the chief's court? His cough had exploded, silencing the whole court. It should not be like that today. This is the day the young blood of the young maiden also flows into his own veins, he knows.

Cattle are soon exchanged between sessions of dance and song. Mafunga, the intermediary, had worked hard day and night. What more does he desire as an intermediary, the bringer-together of two families, the builder of everlasting friendships? He is happy with himself. His face, his eyes, glow in the morning sun. All is well. Good things are good things. You cannot put spices in a gourd of milk – you spoil it, he thinks. Everybody agrees with him, nodding their heads regardless of whether they might fall off with over-nodding or not.

As the evening dew settles on the blades of the dying grass, Mafunga's heart too settles down. Of the frightening visitors of the night, he fears most the jealous witches and wild magicians. They are not always inclined to admire the success of others. He knows they will haunt him night and day, demanding their share of his good fortune. But he consoles himself. A man who is bewitched for his success dies a happy man. Mafunga sighs at this thought. He hears the songs of the distant birds singing praise to him, thanking him for a job performed in the old ways of the ancestors. A pinch of snuff to calm his nerves. Good snuff, this, he says, were it not for too much *mudhombo*. Good snuff. He dizzily thanks the maker of the powder in her absence. Her ancestors will hear it and pass on to her his appreciation in the earthly pleasures that she will get. Happy and longer days on earth, he thinks in his trance-like enjoyment of the powder.

After a few days, sleep does not arrive with the night in Mafunga's house. The young girl has asked him a question which devours his sleep. She has come across him on her way from the well. At sunset, thorny questions cause sleeplessness, like one stabbed by a spear. A lone cloud hangs loosely in the blue sky, over the nearby Bupwa mountain, the holy sanctuary where walkers should guard against abusive words. 'Why did I come here?' the maiden asks him. 'When will I return to my mother?'

Mafunga does not know how to answer. He blames the aunts of the young girl for not telling her everything, for not telling her that from now on she is someone's wife. She belongs to another totem where she will be tasked with creating new blood. They will sing praise to her whenever a child is born, mentioning her name when they pray to their ancestors. She is their new hearth to bring warmth to the cold homestead. Her people will be proud of her. The fertility of her womb will be celebrated here. *Chikuru umvana, umhandara ishongakamwe.* Virginity fades away like mist, like an echo, the drying well. Child-bearing is all. A woman admiring the fontanel of a child, that is the beauty of womanhood. Birds, cattle, elephants, they obey the laws of their ancestors. They sing praises and dance in their own way, he thinks, without telling the girl.

The young woman, a mere girl learning the ways of the world, dies in her heart. She does not understand the few words Mafunga says to her. She walks away with the load of a gourd of water on her bare head, balanced in the way her mother has taught her.

'I do not want to leave my mother alone.' The girl surprises her hearers. She and Mafunga's wife are grinding *rapoko* on their two grinding stones. 'I am the only girl, and to take such a long visit away from my mother worries me. She will go to the well on her own. She will pound the grain, singing songs of missing me. She will cook alone and do all the work alone. I must go back!' Tariro bursts out, watching the harsh colour of the red *rapoko* in her basket. Blood, she thinks. Blood.

'You will go back to visit some time,' Mafunga's wife is quick in answering her. 'You will visit some time, when there is time,' she adds. 'We all visit our homes. This is your new home.'

Tariro hears the woman's piercing voice drowning the air she breathes. 'But why is your daughter of my age still here?' Tariro wants to know. She wants to know why her sisters, the same age as she, are at home with their mothers. She wants to know why she should not be with her mother, listening to her worries, growing up under the wing of a woman who is alone.

Mafunga's wife stares at her and coughs her usual dry cough. 'Life is not the same for everyone,' she tells the young girl, foaming at the mouth as she envisions her own daughter 'marrying a grave', as she thought of it the day she saw the little girl brought home for this marriage.

In her heart, she knows a young woman who marries such an old man is not too many sunsets from the tears of her man's death. Her parents have no pity for her. The little girl's life is doomed. She will eat sadness every day of her life. She will cry silently for many years. I would not do that to my child. Missing all the joys of courtship at the river, at the well, dancing the mischievous dances of girls out to provoke boys with their love songs. Songs to provoke the boys:

Kana ndikadai kana ndikadai, zvoshamisa.
Kana ndikadai kana ndikadai, zvoshamisa.

She had sung those songs herself, in full view of the boys who saw her expose the hidden parts of her body to provoke them. Far off in the distance, the glimpse which the boys had of her half-naked body sent a fire through their bodies. They ran over to her and the other girls, their blood boiling, their hearts wild. The joy of the girls was in running away, never allowing the boys to come nearer than a safe distance. Oh, how satisfying it was, she thinks to herself. She watches this other girl, whose parents have thrown her away like a torn rag, cutting her days of joy and the pleasures of youth.

The sun sets and rises and sets again. Tariro is not found. Even birds sing the songs which they say Tariro sang as she walked away to no one knows where.

> Lost girl,
> Tariro is missing.
> Lost girl,
> Tariro is missing.
> Lost girl,
> Lost girl,

the doves chorus from the top of the trees.

Her mother mournfully hears the loud-mouthed birds sing monotonously about where Tariro is. Where is Tariro? Where is Tariro? Until the echoes of the birds' voices dizzy her with a silent fear.

In the folktales, old women whisper the story of a maiden who refused to enrich her people. Stories of a young girl who deprived her mother of a cow. She is like a mother who takes away a morsel of food from a child's mouth, they say. A woman who vomits when food drops into her mouth. Shame! Shame! Rivers of shame will drown the owner of such an unlucky womb. A womb which brings forth bandits, priests, murderers and rebels. A woman's womb can be as dry as the plains when the rains refuse to fall.

Tariro does not hear it, though. She is already in far-away places, learning the words of a language she has never dreamt she would learn. She has to learn new names like Phiri, Mwila, Mulenga. She will not have the time to talk about Mafunga, Charamba. Only unfamiliar names are now familiar to her ears. She does not mind, though. She will learn. She who wants to swallow a bone must first ask her throat if it is the right size.

Far away, in this new land, Tariro cannot find her way to the water well. It is another dark place with people whose names for everything she knows are different. The hills, the trees, the insects and birds, all are strange, with new names. She too is a stranger to them. And she is afraid. But no one knows her fear.

My mother, she thinks, and cries every day. My mother. She must not die while I am so far away. I want to see her face, just once, before she dies. My body tells me that I am afraid to be so far away. I am afraid and I cannot hide it. There is nobody to tell that I am afraid. Afraid. That makes me more afraid, she thinks to herself, without anyone to tell those thoughts.

The young girl looks at the people around her, in the city far away from home – they call it Lusaka, North Rhodesia – and wonders. She does not even know how to point in the direction of home. She asks someone to point in the direction of her home for her. Will I one day get there and meet my little brothers, children from the same womb as me? Will I one day see my mother, and the little sisters whom I have never seen? She feels she would like to walk there one day.

The burning longing makes her remember the long, tiresome journey to this strange place, through mountains, across endless plains, cutting across all types of unfamiliar landscape, riding on a rickety lorry, sometimes walking and taking refuge from the dark night of wild animals and snakes in the home of a suspicious-looking headman whose language sounded strange and distant.

And the woman who talks to her about it gazes at the young girl and shakes her head in amazement, then grins like an angry dog and falls silent. Has this girl a worm in her head or something? the woman thinks. Does her head turn round and round? Walking so far away? Why did she leave? the woman wonders, before walking away from the young girl, saying she will be back. She must fetch something important from behind those red walls.

But Tariro does not hear her. She waits for an answer. She is told her home is far away and only those who have money and luck can get there. Not on foot.

Tariro misses the little fights she had with her small brothers, the brutes. She hears their voices in her sleep, asking mother where Tariro is, when she will come back. She sees them all the time, in front of her, like little paper pictures which cannot talk. They stand there, shouting at her, insulting her for running away from them. But when their pictures fade, Tariro thinks she has lost her grip of everything. She cries all the time when the pictures appear to her blurred like the moon behind a thin cloud.

I will return, one day. I will return, she thinks to herself at the railway station where she goes to sleep every night.

'You are a young girl. Don't let the city swallow you.

Find some work to do and you will be a free woman. You can go back to your mother without anyone carrying you as if you were a log,' the woman who is sleeping next to her assures her. She knows the heart of the young girl is a burdened heart.

When I grow up, I will. When I grow up, I will. Tariro remembers how she sang with her friends, far away. She sang those songs with them. She did not think they would come to her in this dream, at this railway station, far away in the land of fear.

1968 – Ritual

At the ritual to thank the ancestors for the ripening of the crops, your father kneels at the doorstep of the hut of his senior wife. It is not long before the reddening sky releases the sun to the earth from the mother of fire where it goes every day to rekindle its fires. It could not wait to show its new reddish glow to the eyes of the earth.

A pot of beer oozes with the white froth of the brew inside it. Men, women, children, people of the same blood, they wait in silence as your father takes the small calabash and draws some beer from the big pot. Their blood has flowed through many veins for endless years. No one knows where it started.

'Draw the beer, a full calabash. Don't let your shivering hands spill it,' his mother instructs him. In her blindness, she has been instructing everybody on the path to reach the ancestors, from the time the grain was ground on the grinding stone to the brewing. 'Make sure the beer is brewed by a woman who has reached the menopause,' she told him. All the ears have been listening to her carefully, like people caught up in a drought and so have to listen whenever there is the sound of thunder in the distance. 'No woman suckling a child must come near the grain reserved for the ancestors. I hope some woman's foolishness and evil ways will not desecrate such an important ritual,' they'd heard her say from the start, her voice arrogant, as she had been known to be since her blindness started years before.

All the eyes gathered follow your father's movements as he feverishly draws the beer, sips and pours some on the cow-dung-plastered floor.

'Go on, say the prayers to the ancestors as I have told you. Don't you remember the names? Say them in the correct order, beginning with your father,' she goes on and on, initiating him in the world of the ancestors, how to speak to them so early in the morning before strangers started announcing their impending arrivals . . .

My fathers,
the fathers of my fathers
and their fathers,
and those who inhabit the skies and the earth:
the crops have been good so far.
The children are in good health.
The women have given us children.

Our children obey us.
The cattle,
the cows are bearing young calves,
in twos and threes.
As for the goats and sheep,
we cannot say more than you can see.
Our pens are full.
Wealth is on our doorstep.
Every drop of rain on our fields
Watered a root which gave us grain.
The soil did not throw away the water.
It seeped through with nourishment in its hand
to the roots below.

Now, this drop of water
which we brew for you
is only to tell you
that the thankless child
gets punished by its parents.
We are strong now,
our bellies are full.
This cob here
shows you the strength of your protection.
Care for the children.
Were it not for you,
we would all be coughing and dying,
if not in our graves.
But you care,
You protect us,
You soothe us

When disasters befall us.
You stand by us
like a bird
protecting its nestlings
and feeding them.
You stand by us
so that in the night
witches and ghosts
do not dance the *jikinya* dance
on our sleeping mats.
You frighten them
with your power,
a power which knows
how to direct rains to our fields,
a power which knows
how to chase away ghosts and wild beasts.

You do it as ancestors,
our only refuge.
An ancestor who fails to protect his children
becomes a thing to laugh at in the village.
What then is this which happened?
Did a hen not lose an egg while you watched?
A child refuses the instructions of its parents—
what sort of child is it?
How can such a child go unpunished?
How will children know
the power of their ancestors
if small boys and girls
can pass water on your heads?

A man of standing is seen by deeds.
He cannot allow owls to perch on his rooftop . . .

Thin sounds of sobbing thread the holy air. Sounds of sobbing from among those gathered. More intense sobs interrupt prayers to the gods and the ancestors. Now, more intensely, fading again, interrupting the prayers all the time. Wails, sobs, wails. Wails and sobs. Wails and sobs. Mournful voices and dying heartbeats. The earth crumbles. Rivers also drown fishermen. Everything crawls on broken legs and wings. No handshakes. No smiles. Death walks on the footpath. You met death on the footpath and did not greet him. Ancestors walked silently without seeing you. Another tear drops. A heart too, drops, falling into an endless pit. A flying mosquito is engulfed by a raging fire. No one hears the screams of the tiny insect burning in the fire. It is another silent ritual.

'Who is crying? I can hear the voice of Tariro's mother!' your grandmother shouts. 'This is unheard-of. Defying the ancestors and their wishes! You cry in this ritual to invite the anger of the ancestors. This is a bad omen. Death. It has never been heard before.' The old woman breaks up the ritual, walking away without the help of her walking stick. She throws her hands in the winds in a disgusted gesture as if all has been lost to the winds.

The old woman mourns the death of a ritual she has performed so many times without anyone questioning her. Blind though she is, she can still cry old tears which frighten her hearers. They are tears of death, they say. Wings of death which she has seen flying across the sky. May the witches and diviners not hear this! The man who farts also faces the foul smell, she curses.

Jeers and mumbles as the ritual breaks up. Silence. The women accuse your mother of failing to control herself in front of the ancestors. 'Why did you send your daughter away if you did not want to cry like this?' they go on, one after the other.

Tariro's mother, her hope is ashes now by the end of all these voices. Cold, dry ashes like those in an abandoned fireplace.

'If the ancestors take away my daughter, I curse them,' your mother says, crying. Everyone is silent now. No one has ever defied the ancestors in the village. But today she orders them to bring back her child, here to her own hut, not to some old man who does not know women of his age group from among whom he must marry. 'No, my child must never return if she returns to the hands of an old man. No, my child was born like everyone else. She must come back to me, not anywhere else . . .'

Then silence, for endless years. She does not mention her child's name again. No one will sing Tariro's name in the game of naming when the children play in the moonlight. She will be silence like her mother. Silent tears.

Your father and mother sit, on opposite sides of the fireplace. The fire is dying, almost cold. Not many words pass across the fire. Words burn also: they cannot cross the fire zone. Words are spilled into the air, then the smoke catches them in mid-air, as if they were mosquitoes. They tumble into the dying fire, burn in a sizzle, and die. Who said words were like stones? You cannot pick them up from the fire and cool them. They are easily melted by the heat of the fire, dying in your eyes. You want to cry to both, to say to them: Father, words are burning! Mother, words are burning in the fire! Your words, like the elders' words, burn in the fire before they reach the ears of the two hearers.

Mother's head is bowed, like one praying. She is sitting there, on the floor, with a tiny twig in her hand, fingering it, scratching the hard cement floor with the stick as young maidens do when young men frighten them with words of love. I lose sleep whenever I think of you. I cannot eat. And when the young maidens hear those burning words, their supple eyes glitter with amusement. Lose sleep? Cannot eat? What sort of man is this who lies for the sake of touching the grass where the king's cattle graze? Then they remember: a man who does not lie does not marry. They pick up a twig, a piece of grass, chew it, scratch the hard ground with it, chew it again, and wonder what they should say to this lover drunk with love. Should they give him a gourd full of the love of their own well or not? They look into his eyes and know what he is waiting for. No, they will not give the young man a gourd of milk yet. He must know that, in order to climb to the top of the mountain, you have to go round and round until you are dizzy. I will talk to you about it tomorrow, they tell the young man. Tomorrow. It is not too long to wait. Perhaps the day after tomorrow. Then the young man pleads, words of worship. I am an orphan without you. When will you come to my parents' home to light the fire of our love? My mother waits every day for you to cook for her, to be her mother, to tell her the stories which your mother told you. Remember those folk tales you told the other children at the *mahumbwe* games? My mother wants to hear them. Give me the water from the waterpot, and I will never drink any other water again. The young man goes on and on, every delay being a potion of poison to his heart. Words are too slow. Hearts are too slow. The earth is too slow. His love is hot and fast. He cries and pleads. I will kill my mother if you want me to. I will go without water for two seasons if you ask me to. I will die if you promise to be near the place of my death. I will wrestle with a phython if the reward is you ... The maiden looks at his heart, bare and naked. She tells him it has to be tomorrow. To run is not to arrive. The tortoise also arrived where the rabbit had arrived the month before. Tomorrow, she says.

And when tomorrow comes, the maiden does not appear at the meeting place. The young man is there, dying of the thirst of the heart. She is there, he thinks. She should be here any time. But she is not there. She is not among the bushes. She is not among the dry leaves of the dying grass. She is not there. Her voice cannot be heard. No one can hear any breathing from the hidden places of the land. Has anyone seen a maiden starved of love near here? Has anyone seen startled birds fly from these bushes? Has anyone seen Nyarai going to the well?

Did anyone hear songs of love in these parts? At that point Nyarai arrives, smiling shyly, not apologizing. She smiles and stands in the distance, far away from him, a distance which is short but long at the same time. The distance of yearning. She stands there and smiles, a little twig in her hands, her teeth tired of chewing it. She stands there and smiles, those milk-white teeth revealing to the young man that he is so foolish. Can't he see that she has been in love with him for so long? Can't he listen to the songs which she has always sung at the play-ground? Songs about this bow-legged young man, leave him for me. The boy with a head like a spear, leave him for me. The boy with a little stammer, I want to start something big with him. Hasn't he heard those songs?

'Go and tell your aunt that the sky has smiled at her,' she says, her milk-white teeth exuding a white flame of guarded love. The young man runs away with joy to tell everybody, everything, the dogs, the cats, the chickens of his homestead. A flame will arrive in this homestead at any time. A flame. The flame of love which burns only the twigs of love. Love.

Your mother sits still, worshipping the gods of her ancestors. She thinks and does not think at the same time. Why worry about thoughts when everything is known? It is only a foolish man who looks at his lover from a distance and says: I am thinking about you.

Your father is wearing one of those Hitler coats which covers his whole body except the head and the toes. He sits there too, silent, thinking about what he should do with this woman who insults the ancestors. This woman who has neither fear nor respect. This woman who stands there and tells the gods to die. He does not know if he too should get a twig from the fire to scratch the floor with. The thin silence of the night needs to be broken with a twig.

'What you did yesterday . . .' He pauses. 'What you did yesterday . . .' He pauses again.

'Yes,' your mother mumbles, not quite audibly, but it is all in the ears. The sound affirms that she knows what she did yesterday. She is not like a drunkard who wakes up the following morning and claims he does not know a thing of what he did yesterday. She is not like that.

'What you did yesterday . . .' Your father goes on and on about what you did yesterday, what you did yesterday, what you did yesterday. 'To think that my fathers and their fathers were there. To think that you have thrown the whole family into the dusty pit.' He begins to run short of words.

'I have pain inside my heart,' your mother tells him right there at the fireplace. The words fly again into the fire, burning as if a forge had just been started. 'You know my pain and pretend that it is not a pain.' She stares at him.

Your father does not answer. He has not been answered. He has a different type of pain inside him. The pain of the ancestors. She has the pain of childbirth. The two do not seem to meet. 'From now on, I will not consider you my wife,' your father says, standing up, towering the fireplace.

'You never have,' your mother nimbly says, her voice

fading into the fire, rekindling the dying fire, making the ashes burn once more.

As your father leaves, his footsteps are steps of a bitter departure. They are of feet torn apart with a new disease brought by the white man in the year of the cattle disease. You hear his voice shouting outside at the children playing. You see him walk like a shadow around the homestead, asking for the axe and the hoe, telling the children to weed the fields or count the cattle, ordering a woman to go bring him some food, demanding that such and such a child should be in the fields, not loitering around doing nothing. You hear the faded voice of your father against the wailing songs of your mother. It occurs to you that the pains between the two are so far apart they will never meet.

That day, your mother does not go out of the house. She sits where she was sitting when your father talked to her. She will be there the whole day, a whole lifetime, looking at her life. She thinks how wasted she is. How the years have left her behind. Everything ages, she says inside her heart. Everything ages. Even stones age . . .

In my youth, I was a dancer. I sang and danced, my voice soaring to the skies, capturing all the village's ears, the sleepy ears, the waking ones. I danced the *jerusarema* dance when, like a whirlwind, it caught the whole land. A wild fire beyond control. The dance came and invaded the whole area like a veld fire. It burnt the hearts of many and broke marriages. You cannot imagine what it was for some of us. It was a dance which made young women abandon their new husbands. Some young men, too, left wife and homestead to intruders and strangers, following the flood of the dance from village to village.

People do not know what a dance is. I remember those days when the dance captured the hearts and minds of many until the white rulers had to stop it. What could they do? If you do not stop a dance like that, everything burns to ashes. The real dancers of *jerusarema* danced night after night, following the trail of the dance from village to village, abandoning their fields and families.

My own friend went like that. We never saw her again when the flames of the dance consumed her. The dance started in our village one night, the drums rumbling and screaming for your soul. My spirit was taken away by the sounds. My friend too, she heard the sound of this new drum and followed it to its source. She sang with the singers and danced with the dancers. She was every-thing. With time, the dance stopped her from eating, from bathing, from loving, from everything that she had wanted to do with her life.

When the dance moved to the next village, she moved away with it, like one carried away by a flooded river. She drowned in the dance, singing and feeling the dance tickle her all over her body, her very soul. From day to day, night to night, she went away with the dancers until she saw she had spent many days away from husband and home. She had abandoned them for this dance of fire. Maybe she was too ashamed to come back. How was she to speak to her angry husband and her tempestuous father?

No, my friend decided to follow the dance until she died. Nobody knows how she died. Stories of the manner of her dance wafted in the winds until they reached our ears. The wind could not kill those beautiful stories. She had become dance itself, the heart of the dance, the fireplace of the dance.

I too was a dancer of the *jerusarema* dance, the wild dance of the drums and the big calabash rattles. When in the dance arena, I felt a fire burn through me as if my veins would burst and splash blood in the dance arena. The spirit of the dance had swallowed me. You don't know that a dance swallows the dancer? It eats into you like a story that can never be put into words. Words are small as ants if you have something big from your heart to say. Words: what are words? They are like little bits of rubbish, feathers floating away in the wind. Dance, music, when it captures your heart, can heal cripples who cannot walk. They forget they are crippled, jump up like that, dance and then realize they are cripples later.

Jerusarema was like that to me, to my friend, the disappeared one, the one whose grave they will never see. Sometimes I wish I had gone with her. Only the thought of the children I have today calms me down and tells me: the ancestors had other plans for you. Were it not for that, I would have lived an unhappy life, thinking that my friend, even in death, is still dancing and fascinating the eyes of the ancestors. Ancestors: they must wonder why they died before the flame of this dance came to their homes.

Taxes? You talk about taxes? During our time, when we were girls with breasts bursting on our chests, before the time of Hikira, taxes were not an issue for the headman. Police came in jeeps and on horseback to collect every man who had not paid tax. They took them to *chibharo* camps where men were forced to work until they had earned enough money. One shilling, two shillings for the angry District Commissioner. In the mines, in the wide fields of greedy farmers, on the roads, building bridges alongside Italian foremen, everywhere.

When *jerusarema* came, even the men who had wanted to avoid annoying the white man had to abandon all plans to go to Jo'burg to work and raise taxes for the white man. They refused and fought back when the white man came to capture them to put them to work on the roads and in the mines. Some went to hide in the mountains and hills during the day and came out at night to dance *jerusarema* with the women and men of the village.

So the white man sat down one day and said: this dance is another problem. We must stop it. The dance gives too much pride to these men who refuse to work in our mines and on our roads. We must stop it forever. Never to be danced again. Never again to hear the songs which start this dance. Death to anyone who sings the songs. Death to anyone who dances the dance.

That is how *jerusarema* was killed. We only hear of it in distant parts these days. In Murewa, maybe Mutoko, no one knows. I don't know where that is, but I hear the drums every day in my inner ears. The drums of my youth.

A sad thing happened during this time of *jerusarema*. I was a dancer, graceful and careless in the dance arena. My ageing father saw me dance one day. He cried: What have I brought to this earth? What has the stomach of a woman brought to this earth? What has the stomach of a woman brought to this earth? he cried. Then he called me one day to his hut and scolded me about this provocative dance. Who did I want to provoke with this dance so full of movement and sexual stories? Who do you want to provoke? You danced that dance, all the eyes of the village looking. You make their hearts wear out in search of you. Whose daughter is this? 'I will bring the cattle tomorrow morning if only she says yes this night.' Where did you learn this dance, child? My father was angry.

My father then met with strange men and women, talked in a language I did not know. Soon, aunts and relatives came to fetch me as if I was a goat on sale. They washed me up, dressed me up in the newest skins they could find and took me away.

We walked away from my mother's house, silent as if they were taking me for a sacrifice. My heart told me my father had asked them to kill me. He had been a warrior of Mzilikazi and Lobengula. Killing a man had not been difficult for him. As for a small girl like me, I am sure it would have been like swallowing saliva for him. No pain. No tears.

After a short walk, we stopped at a homestead which I knew very well. It was the homestead of one who had grown so friendly with my father people thought they were brothers.

The owner of the homestead came out and whispered something to the men and women who had brought me. A few women from the homestead came out and started ululating, dancing with their bare feet, wriggling their waists like crocodiles slithering on the sand. They said how beautiful I was, what a wife I would become, how great the homestead I came from, how everything was smooth as the waters flowing in the valley.

Only the wife of the man who was to be my husband looked hurt. I felt her eyes push me against a rock, telling me to go home where I came from. I was afraid.

The carver of stools and drums became my husband from that day on. I could not run away. Where could I go? My father was known for his Ndebele ways. If I ran away, my own mother, who had died when I was a tiny girl, would have a curse on her grave. I decided to stay. The men of the village, the women too, had told me that the carver of the stools, drums and snuff horns was a wonderful man. Everybody told stories of how he made rain, and how he had such power in him that even the headman feared him. A peaceful man full of love, they said. He was only unlucky enough to have a wife who shouted at him and did not see the powers that the ancestors had given her husband.

I decided to stay until my womb was ripe to receive his seed. One after another, the children came. A girl, a boy, and another boy. When I was pregnant with the third child, the carver of the wood fell ill and died. He had sung and danced the whole night, perched on his favourite tree with his drum. The whole village was shaken by the rumble of his voice and the thunder of his drum. Then he died early the following morning, before the red sun came to mourn him. That day, a red sun crossed the sky for me, like a flame hanging up there in the sky. I was alone now, the sun said to me. Only memories remained of how he asked me to be his wife, how he asked me to prepare tobacco for him, how he told me if I did not want him to be my husband, I could leave him or stay with him until I found a young man of my choice. Memories of how he took large pinches of snuff and asked the gods to bring rains.

I remember one day he had been possessed by the spirit of the drum. He climbed a huge tree, singing for the rains to come, in the middle of the dry season. There, out there, small clouds gathered and drifted to our homestead. In the midst of the dry season, rain fell until we were all drenched.

My husband was a man who spoke with the gods. We became so close he was like my father. After he died, I could not stop crying for a long time. He had been my father and guide although I had not initially wanted to be married to him. He was old. My father's age. Even now, I hear voices from his many voices. I hear him call me by my name. I cannot stop listening to him. He tells me to go on when I have problems. He tells me he is with me all the time, waiting for me to join him, telling me to get out of this and that danger. He is still my husband . . .

Your mother remembers the silent stories of things you do not understand. She talks and gives up all the time. No one listens and she feels hurt because she thinks no one hears her stories.

1920 – *Carver*

In my deafness, my dumbness, I was also a hearer. I heard because my eyes saw, heard and spoke. No one listened. Those who have a mouth, an ear sitting on either side of their heads, and tongues dancing in their mouths, sometimes do not hear or talk. I was one of the hearers. Alone, like a lonely bird flying in the empty sky. I was alone, with eyes to fight with, nothing else. Imagine, the sounds of the birds were all darkness to me, though I could see birds perched up in the trees, colourful beaks and feathers, making dances for their lovers without me hearing their music. Insects, fireflies. Singers at the *mahumbwe* dance, gracefully embracing the sky and the wind, moving this way and that, gesturing to a young man or woman, then bowing to take someone's daughter in marriage. I did not hear them. Darkness surrounded me like a mist.

Before all of you were born, a carver of stools, drums and snuff horns was born. He carved under the *musuma* tree, singing with the joy of what he saw in the wood, insulting his neigbours in a way which made them laugh, provoking them as they passed by, saying to him: This mad one will be like that till he dies. 'Carver of drums and other things, what are you carving today?' they asked, on their way to the nearest beer drink.

'Did you think I was carving your mother's breasts? This is a drum, if your eyes are blinded by the thirst. You play drums and dance your madness at the beer party: do you think the drums fall from the sky like showers of rain?' The inquirer laughs himself hoarse, watching closely the fingers of the carver holding on to a sharp piece of metal whose name the onlooker does not know, carving hands, sweating lips, carving, the face of the carver telling stories of a dance delayed, life created anew in song and dance, the thrill of a voice never before heard in the whole village. A dance with wings, flying, perching, not perching, wild, now calm, frenzied, a dance that rises and falls at the same time. A dance that talks of colours of the pain in the hearts of men and women who have not even spoken. Children whose tongues do not even have words stuck to them. A dance that flies and perches, like a tired firefly.

This drum should have been ready for the harvest dance before the full moon. My slow hands! Had the white man not kidnapped me to go and work in his mines, I should have finished it and delivered it to its owner. You know, this drum is worth a cow, the face of the man says. Dancers will see their ancestors, their souls, in this drum, he thinks.

The watcher sees the pain in the man's heart. He hears

the echoes of voices of singers at the ceremony, the *bira*. He can see the intensity of the carver on the ageing fingers and wrinkled face. Many years of carving drums, horns and stools have made the man's face shrink like an old blanket.

Many faces meet in one face. A song. A whistle. Another tragic dance. A pattern of dancing feet, and hands weaving a dance in the air. Many songs from the drum and the *kudu* horn that will be blown until the neighbouring villages all assemble for the ritual of the ancestors. A voice echoing in distant hills. The horn, too, tells stories of desertion and love, hatred flooding the heart like a river, invitations to love, war and death.

Far-away places come together in song and dance, the yearnings and desires of the hearts of the dead and the living, all in one whirlwind.

A carver of horns and drums and stools was born before any of you was born. Miriro once again tells her story. She wants me to hear who lived in this village, our village, our blood. We borrowed these dreams from him. The blood and breath of a carver of wood, she says in a whisper, are in you.

The carver of wood did not have too many words for our ears. He said what he had to say and went back to his carving. Words were like feathers to him. Only his carving mattered. He talked to the carvings, whispering to them, caressing them like the sweaty body of a lover. No words for your ears. No words for passers-by. His mouth must rest so his heart can speak in a thunderous silence.

Silence is not a sign of foolishness. The drums were not silent. Many villagers danced till their feet cracked, playing the drums created by the carver of drums. I know you were too far in your mother's womb to hear the rumble of the drums. To hear the voice of the horns he carved with his own hands. To sit on the wooden stools on which were carved the totems of those who sat on them. The monkey totem, the fish eagle, which he saw flying gracefully in the sky, the elephant, massive and clumsy, the zebra, the snake totem, which he carved and felt would bite anyone who came near it. Maybe you saw some of the drums, which lasted endless years. He made them to last forever so they could throb in the hearts of those whose hands played them.

Then one day he climbed a huge tree, the *musuma* tree, his favourite one, after he had finished carving his last drum. He took the drum with him up there into the sky, singing sorrowful songs. Pain flooded the whole valley with his voice. Joy, too. He knew the pain and joy in the drum. He had lived them all his life. You saw them on his face as he carved. He carved and carved and carved, saying all the names of the ancestors who gave him the dream to carve wood, to make wood talk, to make wood sing and dance, to make dead wood come back to life again with leaves and flowers.

The carver climbed the tree with the huge drum, started singing aloud like one wailing, crying for the departed ones. He sang until the whole village came to see and hear him up there in the tree, perched, like an eagle, on his feet.

He sang about life and death, about marriage and the mischief of wives and husbands, about the misfortunes of the world and the joys of defying the gods and the ancestors. Everyone stared at him. No one dared ask him to come down. He sang louder and louder as if his voice would echo from the roof of the sky. Louder and louder and louder, a supple voice that went into the hearts of all. Then everyone joined in and danced in a new ritual which they had never seen in their lives. Children, women, young and old, men, boys and girls, everybody, the priests and the witches, young men who did not know the smell of the mature body of a woman, maidens who still went to the well searching for love, singing and dancing as they stared at their images in the water of the well. They sang and danced until they all cried with the pain of joy. The carver went on singing, dancing, his voice soaring into the air like a bird freed from the hands of a hungry man.

Dark clouds gathered. First in patches, then darker and darker like thick blankets. Then came the downpour, drenching everyone, the sky and the earth, all merged in the streams of the sky.

Rain fell that day. Rain with thunder but no lightning. It fell and all the rivers and streams said, yes, we agree to be flooded with this muddy water. Still the carver went on singing, playing the drum in the rain, everyone dancing, singing, itching with life and death, joy and sorrow, every sore bared, veins of life open, flooding everyone.

The following day, early in the morning, before the

sun even dreamt of rising, he called his sons, including the little one who was still to be born. He called them to his side and told them what he had in front of him. Death. I did not live in greed. I do not die in greed. If any one of you does not know how to share with his own blood, he will live a life of pain. He told them that everything he had was for all of them. The rain falls for us all, old and young, he said.

With the early-morning birds beginning to sing, he called his two wives, one very old, the other young, almost a child, to him. They sat by his mat of death, listening to his words. The children, he said, treat them with great care. I did not leave them much, but it does not matter. Wealth is in their hands. Only feet and hands can explore new dreams, he said. Buttocks can never discover new lands. When they cry, teach them to wipe away their tears, to laugh before the sun sets so they do not sleep with anger on their sleeping mats. Kindness is the father of love, he said. Tell them to hear the voices of passers-by who will say: How are the children of the carver?

As the cock crowed, the breath of the carver of wood escaped from his mouth forever. No voice would be heard from his lips again. No one would pass by to see him carve again. No new drums would rumble to the tune of ceremonial elders as they sang in praise of his drum again. No dust would rise from the earth in the dance of the ancestors. Nothing. Only silence and echoes coming from those who remembered the carver of wood, the carver of drums and snuff horns, the one who made the forest tremble with song and dance, rising, like smoke, from the drums of his hands . . .

Miriro, the deaf-and-dumb one, speaks to no ears. The hearers are sleeping, drunk with the pleasures of their own hearts, drowned by the flood of their own sweat.

I will not tell you about the way he was buried, she says. Even the white man who had captured the carver of drums once for refusing to work for him, he came to see where the carver of drums was buried. The wails of the women and the tears of the men went with him deep down into the earth. The sore chests of women still remember the carver of wood. The tears on the faces of the men still remember the day the carver of wood departed . . .

Miriro says she will be silent. She speaks to me and asks me to tell the story to those who can hear.

The carver of drums, stools and snuff horns. I hear Miriro's voice every day and night, singing, her feet dancing in the hot dust, her voice worn out with anguish. May she pick up a flower in the field and swallow it for her comfort!

Omen

A few months after the failed ritual, your father walks in the fields, feeling the pulse of the crops in him. He hears persistent yells from the homestead. He listens intently to see if he can discern the wailing voices.

No, the wind is blowing in the wrong direction. He walks again, touches the blades of the leaves of the maize plants, green and brittle. He smells the cotton plants, the leaves juicy but smelling of the hot powders which are sprayed to scare away the insects or kill them.

Your father is walking in the direction of home, thinking what this woman thinks she is that she can pour sand in the face of his ancestors. He sees her packing her belongings, a few clothes and pots, walking away never to return again. He spits on the soft earth and watches the soil and the air swallow the blotch of saliva. Vanishing.

It is ten years now since his mother has been blind. She knows how to walk the compound without a leading hand. She says what pains her all the time. There are things she does not say, he thinks. Things which he also knows. She will die without telling them to anyone else except himself.

The carver of wood had told her everything that was in his heart. She had told it to him as well. The carver had also told him and a few others. It does not matter any more now, he says in the silence. It does not matter at all.

Still the wailing gets nearer and nearer as the wind changes direction. It must be something serious. He had thought it must be some jealous woman who had taken to her grinding stone and started pouring out the burdens of her heart for all to hear. It has happened before. Women and their songs, he had thought.

But now he has to hurry home. Since it is getting dark,

maybe someone searched for him in the wide fields and failed to find him. The land of Gotami gives you crops the size of forests, he thinks to himself.

'She is dead,' the senior wife tells him, standing outside the hut where his mother had stayed since blindness attacked her. 'She is dead,' the woman tells the man, her voice full of tears of death.

After tears and sorrow, your father does not whisper any more some of the tales of death. I know the person who did it, he says. I know, he says. That woman has to go to the home of her fathers. I have already told her she is no longer my wife. She will have to go. Her hand is the hand of death. You hear the words all over the place, in the air, among the cattle and sheep, from the mouths of the maize plants.

Your mother sits there and thinks, silent too, like Miriro. The journey to the lands of Gotami reaches far, she sighs.

1989 – Wounds and Smiles

It is not easy to tell this story of a deaf-and-dumb woman married in her deafness, her inner silences, eternal.

The land smiles sometimes, but at times it is sadly mourning. Sad when that which the land does not wish is born. Smiling when mothers sing lullabies to babies that are born with ears, eyes, noses, legs, fingers. It was like that in those lands when memory was no longer useful for remembering things. People only looked and said: *that one*. They were stilled to silence, hurt inside their hearts and memories. *That one*: that was where it all ended. Words failed to carry burdens stored in the hearts of the young and the old.

How do you point at a cripple and say, this is a cripple, without legs and fingers? This is a cripple who, if left alone, would not do anything for themselves. Many came to watch the sight of this cripple. Oh, how the ancestors can punish the living! Oh, how the gods sometimes want to show us the way to live on this earth! This is not alone. This surely is a bad omen. The earth gets angry at times and darkness eats into you during the day. It has to be so. Onlookers need a story to retell the following day or in the dark corners of the night.

In the end, nothing is hidden from eyes, ears, from memory. Even you yourself are an onlooker, watching your own story. Everything becomes the property of everyone, voices becoming the property of all who have faces and mouths, songs becoming the property of all who can sing or hear them in their silence.

'Why did I get married?' Miriro asks. This is the girl who does not even know her name. She does not know it because the ancestors and the gods sealed her ears, her mouth too.

Miriro cannot ask these questions of her fathers, the ones who one day sat under the *muonde* fruit tree, gestured in her direction for so long, grinned with pity for her and nodded. They went on and on, as if their lips were calling her and wanting to ask her what she thought of the sun and all its branches which gleam on the green blades of the wild grass. It had been so all her life. The gleam of the sun on the leaves. The blinding rays flooding her face, frightening her. She had seen the fingers of the women pointing at the water pot. Then she had taken the water pot to the well, to see her sister, the mad one, dance around the well and sing as she admired her naked breasts:

> '*Ah, hinga ndakanaka!*
> *Ah, hinga ndakanaka!*
> *Ah, hinga ndakanaka!*'
> 'Oh, how beautiful I am!
> Oh, how beautiful I am
> Oh, how beautiful I am!'

Miriro only sees the lips and the dance, feeling it filter into her own breast like a fresh wind blowing in the hot sun. She does not hear the words of the girl who sings to tell herself that she is a maiden: may the world watch and see what she will do to the hearts of men?

Miriro had been so named to say to the ancestors, we will wait for the day when this woman, glamorous, beautiful, can speak, sing the songs of the land which are bursting in her heart and hear the music of birds flapping their wings in the sky. *Ah, hinga ndakanaka!* she should sing one day at the well, celebrating the gracefulness of her body and the wonder in her voice. So they gave her a name to challenge the ancestors, the gods. Give a voice to this beautiful maiden. Give ears to this beauty of the land. They say sweetness comes with sand in it so that people do not drown themselves in it. The honey that is sweetest comes with pebbles of sand so the taster can enjoy only rumours of the sweetness. Honey which comes without sand or pieces of bark in it is always full of death, they say. Eaters of such honey drown their souls in it and forget the ancestors.

But this honey had too much sand in it, they said. Miriro, deaf, dumb. No words ever to tickle the inner corners of her soul. Deaf. Dumb.

Miriro, the one the whole village is waiting to speak, they married off to a man she did not love. From that day, in protest, she did not want to look at the faces of those around her. Her eyes were cast to the ground. She did not smile any more at those who looked shyly at her face. She became a ghost, like those ogres, the *goritoto*, hidden away in the jungle, waiting to pounce on the night walkers, especially small children who could be gobbled down the throat in one mouthful without a fight. The ogres were still in the minds of the children from the previous night's stories, romping around the land, plundering, killing, eating the uneatable, crushing left-over bones so the villagers should know that they meant what the stories said about them. Ghosts hungry for human blood and breath, everything, munching the visible and the invisible in the darkness of the night.

Early one cold morning, they woke up and found Miriro a mere ghost, dead. She had not said a word or sung a song of the sorrows of her heart the previous night. She had just died and left all words unsaid. Those who could speak sent word of this omen of worse things to follow.

A young woman, before her womb could nurture a seed, taking her own life. They wondered.

After burying her, they go to diviners and medicine-men to cleanse the village. Their memories, too, need to be cleansed. So the diviners sprinkle them with herbs, water, concoctions, flavours, incantations. Silence follows, and the comfort of knowing that death is painful but some deaths are welcome. They remove burdens from the living and the dead.

Endless years pass. The names of the ancestors fade slowly from the minds of the living. The skies too change. The seasons begin to cry. No clouds. No rains. No gleaming blades of grass in the plains and the valleys. The rain-bird is as silent as death.

'There is a woman who died, silent, in your family many years before any of you were born. So don't try to remember. The memory is mine.' The diviner looks at the beads in her palms. 'I can see it. She died silently, but do you think a person who dies a silent death has nothing to say? She died silently like a piece of wood. You should have been there to see the face of her death. But you were not born. Your own fathers and mothers had not seen the face of the sun. You did not know the faces of your ancestors. They were there, and they made her kill herself.' The diviner goes on and on, words pouring from her mouth, the beads in her palm glittering in the half-darkness of a slow-glowing fire. 'The voices of the silent are painful when they come to the living,' she says, full of sorrow for the visitors. Her body is writhing with the pain of this divination. She is like one engulfed in a flame that only she can see. Her eyes, which see the invisible, see beyond the years, everywhere. No one answers her.

Months later, your father sits alone and remembers. I don't know what the deaf-and-dumb woman wants, he says to himself. She comes in dreams and diviners' beads. She makes everyone cry, he thinks, then remembers how his own father, the carver of wood, told him the sad story of this woman who, deaf and dumb, lived a short and sad life. She was a woman with breasts already the size of small pumpkins. No one would marry her. She was to be pitied. No one ever felt he could be her husband. A silent life, pointing at things and mumbling through life. No, the men said.

Then one day a man, drunk and worthless, passes by, staggering home through the village. 'The silent one! The silent one!' the man shouts. Then: 'I will marry the silent one. The one everybody despises. Give her to me,' the drunk shouts, singing about his broken loves and burdened heart.

The following day the man comes again with his words. He will marry the silent one. For him, an old woman is a wife. It is not the same as sleeping on a cold mat.

The elders sit under the big *muonde* tree, point in Miriro's direction, nod their heads, and the next thing she is on her way to a home she does not know. She walks, thinking what no one will ever know. Those who have taken her to her husband come back with smiles on their faces. She will do well, they say. She works hard as a woman. What more does a man need in a wife? They talk and cast away any memories that might disturb them in their days of suffering and happiness.

When a few days later she has taken her own life, with her own hands, the elders sit again and cry: nothing like this has ever happened in our blood. Nothing. They shake their heads, silence descending upon them like a cloud of smoke.

Part 3

Children

1963 – Hearers of Tales

YOU SIT AND LISTEN to the fearsome hooting of the night owl. As the night gets darker, the voice of the night owl gets nearer and nearer, haunting you like a nightmare. You will not hear the silent voice of Miriro, the woman who is also a dream, like the voice of the owl. Your father asks you to rekindle the fire. A fire prepared by men must not resemble a firefly. A little flame that eats itself to death. *Moto wemadhodha negauvirire.* The flame of men must burn wild. Burn the earth. The silence of Miriro's voice, the silence of Tariro's voice, wherever she may be, is not heard. You listen to the tales of your father. I, the dream, am a hearer, a mere listener, like the animals and trees you always thought were silent . . .

Once upon a time, your father begins, a man fell in love with a lady teacher. The man was really in love, and the woman so beautiful, so beautiful that most men had no courage to approach her. Have you ever seen a woman who is so beautiful that when she looks at you at night, it is as if the moon had given out all its light and

• 151 •

said to the sun, you will not be needed tomorrow? I have taken the day and the night away from you. The woman was like that. Mambi, the man, suffered every day as he stared at this woman. He was not at all ugly, but he was not educated. His father had not allowed him to go to school. There was no one to take care of the cattle. That was the worst part of it. The man could not write.

Mambi decided that a man must die trying. In a fight, a man can be said to be dead only when flies perch on his intestines. Have you not heard what a short man can do in a fight? A blazing fire, a whirlwind of anger. Love too is a whirlwind. The cripple has his own plans for survival.

'Hey, my friend, I cannot sleep. The beauty of this woman is so bewitching. I close my eyes at night. Birds, insects, crickets, cicadas mock me. Pebbles of sand stare at me and laugh during the day. The sky falls, the fruit tree gets taller and taller beyond my reach when I am hungry. Life. Death. Love is death by pain. Do you think you can write a letter for me? Cursive script. Letters that flow like water in the valley. Flowers of my desires. My thirst. In words which the white man has learned how to pin down on a piece of paper. Words which fly with their own wings. Singing words. Yearning words, pleading to the woman, her beauty. A letter. You know I cannot write,' Mambi begged his friend.

The friend, a kind man, explained the danger of pretending. One must keep one's desires to one's own size. A cripple must not aspire to climb the highest mountain. It is a wise cripple who dances leaning against a wall.

Mambi could not accept those words. He wished he could accept them as words of wisdom. Isn't wisdom, in times of love, foolishness? But his heart forbade him what his head said yes to. A man must die trying, even if there may be problems.

'It is I who will face the problems. The problems I am facing now are so big that I cannot postpone the solution in the hope that tomorrow I will be happy. I cannot do that,' Mambi insisted. 'A man who consoles himself with yesterday's pleasures is a foolish man.'

'I hear your words. I will write the letter for you.' His friend yielded.

It was not long before a boy, on bare feet, wearing a loincloth, delivered a letter to the woman. A letter, in the best cursive script, the best curls, clean ink on paper as green as the new leaves in the forest.

The hearth of my home will glow with life only when you enter my house. For now, there is the darkness of a night without stars. No wonder people ask me, why are you getting thinner and thinner each day? Has food run short in your house? I look at them and say: It is the soil which knows that a tortoise's baby is ill.

The woman marvels at this man who writes such beautiful letters, pleading, joking, provoking, amusing.

Several letters later, a reply came from the woman, written with humility and love.

My aunt already knows I have finally arrived at the

destination of my heart's desires. I have you and you have me. Come home to arrange with my aunt how the daughters of our village are married. Before the sun hides under the tall trees, I will wait for you under the *muhacha* tree. Just whistle when you get there. I will appear from somewhere to greet you before you see my aunt. Come quickly. Only the heart knows how its pain is caused. Mine is a bleeding heart. All I do is look and say: I cannot die of thirst when my feet are immersed in the river water.

Mambi walked across the valleys and mountains, rivers and forests, pleading, only armed with the desires of his heart, the unending passions which flowed out of him like water from a spring.

After a few days, an intermediary was already wearing out his tyre sandals every day, carrying endless words, messages. And Mambi was receiving letter after letter, strange foods cooked from the recipes the woman had learnt from the white man's books. Everything was as smooth-flowing as the water in the valley. Gentle, calm, moving ahead without any disturbance.

Soon everything which had to be done to bring the new wife home was done. The woman was soon cooking for Mambi, a happy man.

He walked with her to the water well so that greedy men could not steal her from him. A happy man, he boasted about the beauty of the woman in his home. A happy man, he sang her name in his dreams, at the beer parties, at work parties. Where could he go without either taking her with him or returning early for her? The woman of my desires must not feel lonely. She will think of her mother, far away from where I took her, the man went on.

It was not long before problems arose. A letter came from the woman's village. Mambi, still hiding his inability to read, received the letter, opened it and glanced at it in serious silence. Then he exploded in fits of laughter, his saliva splashing the walls of the house. 'Hahahaha, this man! How can he write such funny stories? Woman, I tell you, those who cannot read do not know what the world is all about. Look at this! Look at this! Hahahahaha! Let me laugh while I am in good health.' Mambi went on and on, praising the white man for bringing this new dream of writing and reading, the skill of carrying words on a little piece of cloth from one village to another, from the sky to the earth.

The woman, thrilled by the pleasure in the eyes of her husband, moved nearer, feeling the warmth of the man's thigh, to read the letter so full of laughter. Her face was glowing with anticipation.

Ah, ah, are those not tears welling up in her eyes? The woman sobbed and wailed, her wails flooding all the hills and caves nearby and far away. Oh, how did I marry such a heartless man, with a piece of stone for a heart? A man who laughs at my own father's death! 'You laugh at this letter? You laugh at my father's death' The woman curses the man, her heart sore like one burnt by hot ashes in the soles of the feet.

With a curse, a marriage ended. The storyteller, too, ended.

Your father ends the story and smiles.

The story has taken your soul. You do not hear the night owl any more.

In the dark night, the flames flicked from the fire. You sat quietly, seeing your father's face. You did not see another hearer of these tales. You did not hear Miriro asking your father, in a silent voice: Where is Tariro? Your father did not answer. He stood up and walked away, in the dark, to sleep and dream. But sleep did not come to him. You, too, became a dream which cries.

1964 – Potions for a New Home

Catch a lizard, the one that slithers on the walls of the hut and refuses to go into the forest or the caves of the rocks. Kill it without spilling its blood, and cut off its tail. Throw away the rest of the body and keep the tail only. Dry the tail carefully in the sun or by the fire at night when no one can see you. Hide it all the time, from all eyes and all ears. Grind the dried lizard's tail, and secretly administer it with food to all you would like to be part of your permanent household: wives first, then children, servants if necessary. No one shall ever betray thee.

Kill a snake, especially the vicious cobra. Cut off its tail and tie it to a long string. Drag it around the homestead. Ask someone to come behind you, cursing at the cobra's tail and at all the snakes of the land and daring them to come to your homestead. With a small whip, he must strike at the tail gently all the time as you go round and round the homestead until the tail is worn out. No snake shall ever attack thee, man or serpent.

Search the forests in the dry season for a large tortoise, not the small one which does not appear in the folktales. The really large one, the size of a small boulder. Bring it home alive. Dig a deep hole at the centre of the homestead and bury it there alive, under a shady tree. Nothing will ever crumble in this homestead.

After every harvest, offer prayers to your ancestors even if the rains have been bad. Do not hesitate to insult and scold the ancestors if they have not performed their duties well. Thou shalt not be like the crow which ate and rubbed its beak in the dust and forgot.

Find a feather from an owl and burn it in the homestead at night. All the time tell the owl, through its feathers, that this is not a homestead where it may dance on the rooftops and the trees nearby. No owl will ever perch on your roof. And witches, too, will fear you till you die.

Inside the cattle pen, bury the sharp spines of a porcupine at sunset as the children drive the cattle inside the pen. No cattle will ever leave your cattle pen.

Smear the fat from a lion's carcase on your body – the forehead, the chest, the knees and the elbows. Do it early in the morning before other people wake up. Thou shalt be feared by both the dead and the living.

Smear the fat from a dead python on your body. Thou shalt live a long time.

1967 – Little Loves

Then you feel you are already a man, with this rebellious body in your body, a new discovery. You feel something different in you, a new thorn whose pain you do not understand. The whole body wants to rebel against itself. At night the dreams change. They are no longer the fears about father whipping you for losing a goat or a cow. They are different. The girl who plays netball appears in your dreams, like a welcome apparition, in her green uniform, her thighs exposed to your eyes only. You see the patterns of little patches of lucky dust on her dark thighs and feel the whole world meets where the dust and the flesh of her thighs meet. She even touches you after netting the ball in a netball game, holding your hand, defying the schoolteacher right before her eyes. Every night, every dream, she is there with her wild, rebellious ears and bracket-like legs. Her voice only shouts for the netball to be passed to her, not to you to come to her. It causes you nightmares to know that. She sings loudest after scoring for her school, dancing too, with her waist twisting wastefully regardless of the netball teacher's censure.

At last you find a piece of paper to pull out from your school exercise book. A letter has to be written. A good proposal of love must be consummated by a letter, with the help of the *Oxford Dictionary* and the *Students' Companion*. 'Dear Sinet, Ian Smith can die one hundred times, the land can be flooded by the seas, the droughts can come one after another until the soil is all rock, and God can walk barefoot on this land of Gotami; I will still love you.' You send an emissary to put the letter somewhere where she will obviously see it.

The girl with erect breasts does not answer your letter. You see her every day, walking past you, giving you a provocative glance with an eye which tells you she has noticed your love. Your body is still as hot as the fireplace of love, the forge where love was made. You cannot add sums in school and the teacher is angry with you. Whenever you fail to add simple sums, the teacher makes annoying remarks about some people wanting to run away from school to get married, but you don't even hear the voice of the teacher. It is the girl's voice you hear.

Finally, when no reply comes, you decide to write again. 'Dear Sinet, These days I cannot go to Sunday school. The idea of you being my lover has taken over the place of Sunday school. The place reserved for God in my mind and heart has been taken over by you. I don't mind what your mother and father think about this. You should not even think about them. Love has no father and mother except you and me. It has no God except you and me. My love for you is longer than the Mississippi and higher than Mt Everest . . .'

You send the letter to her by slipping it in her essay

book. A day or two later, your father calls you with a voice full of anger. 'You are no longer going to school from now on. You want to marry, don't you? Married people like me stay at home. This letter you wrote with your own hands, telling her that her father and God and the ancestors are useless when it comes to your love for this girl . . .' Your father looks at you with a stern eye. You can only look at the hard earth and cry amorous tears of shame. To think that such intimate secrets should be in the hands of those who do not deserve to see them! To think that such letters almost always get lost, ending up in the wrong hands! The letter has another letter to accompany it from the girl's father.

As soon as you see that letter, you already think of the eyes of the school on you. The whole flood of eyes at the morning assembly, when the head teacher announces that you want to leave school to marry this girl. You feel betrayed by everything, the land and the air. In your heart you wish you could write a letter to the head teacher to say, please, do not do this. Do not tell everyone in the school. My father, don't write the letter, because you hope that no one has told the head teacher.

In the morning, the head teacher inspects you at morning assembly. Everybody is clean except for the dust-covered bare feet. When he stands erect in front of the schoolchildren, you know that the time to die has come. 'Mucha and Sinet, please come forward,' he says, straightening his tie and wiping the little early-morning sweat from his face.

You step forward. The girl steps forward. In front of

all the children, some of them already men and women with thick voices and breasts as large as gourds. Your heart has already died when the teacher tells the whole school that you have declared your intention to marry this girl, that school is no longer useful for you. You don't hear it when the whole school laughs at your tears. It is as if the blood of your body has spilled and everyone in the school is washing their hands in it, laughing at you, defying your heart, your face, everything. You cannot even see your friend's eyes, so full of sympathy for you, as he tells you later.

After that death, you and the girl are only ghosts in the school. She does not play netball so well any more. You cannot concentrate on schoolwork any more. You want to run away from everyone you see. Whenever her eyes meet yours, you think she says she hates you more than death itself.

The days of suffering have been many. One day she meets you on her way from Sunday school. She does not talk much with you. She moves near to you and whispers: 'Don't worry about your letter,' and runs away to her mother's hut, where she is already late.

April 197 –

Dear Brother Fanwell
As I sit in the half-light to write this letter, mother is standing, towering over me, as if she could show me how to

write. This is her letter to you. She says she would have walked the whole way to come and speak with you about her life and the life of the smaller children whom she worries about so much more than anything else. Frail as she has been these days, I persuaded her that she can send a letter instead of walking and falling on the doorstep at your work. She is looking at these words as if she ever saw the doors of a school, to make sure I write this letter as she wants it written. You know how I removed some of her words the other time when she wanted to ask for money from you? She is careful now . . .

Tell him, she says, I want to know what makes you want to grow white hair on your head without a wife. It is not that I love grandchildren (and what is wrong with that?), but that if you marry, you can build a home of your own somewhere. I will then be able to come and stay with you.

You might say, ah, this old woman's madness is back again. You can open your mouth until dust and soot gather there, in surprise, but the truth is that the sky is no longer the same where I and the children are. The journey which made us leave the home of our birth seems not to end. It goes on and on like the journey of a madman, a wayfarer, who roams the land until he dies by the side of the footpath.

Things are not right for me and the children, I have told you this. Maybe you plug your ears with sticks. Soon I will be sent away. Where do I go? What do I do with these children? I cannot swallow them back into my womb. They cannot help themselves. None of them is big enough to work and earn money to send the others to school.

I don't know what the white man gives you so that you can work for him, sleeping in the wild forests for him. Maybe you tasted soup made from money, I don't know. For me, I want only a home for these children, not money. If you do not have a woman who wants to marry you, I can find a medicine-man tomorrow to cleanse you of that bad luck. If you do not build a home of your own soon, my death will be a miserable one. You will look at my grave and say: This is an angry traveller who died on my doorstep. Look at the beard on your face, do you think it is a sign of being crippled?

If I die in a bad way, with these wounds in my heart, it is not good for you, your children and the children of their children. You know the anger of a woman after death. It can finish you all. If your ears cannot listen, take a piece of cotton wool and clean them. I want you to come and talk to me about these things. I am doing this so that you will be removed from the path of shame. How shameful it will be when your brothers, children from the same womb as you, are seen walking on the roads of Gotami's people's land, carrying dirty bundles on their heads like migrant cotton pickers, bare feet and tattered clothes, with nowhere to go. What a shame it will be even for you at your work! Is that something you can laugh about when you talk to your friends where you work? Even the white man will laugh at you as he drinks his tea after you have made it for him. This man makes such good tea, but where is his life going? the white man will say with his own mouth when he sees what is about to happen.

I am telling you that my eye sees too many things

happening. I am not a baby who smiles at an angry lion coming with its jaws wide open to swallow it. When you look at the whiteness on my head, it is not as if I had been carrying a bag of mealie-meal. It is age. I know danger and shame when I see them.

If you don't go to a headman to look for a place to build a home now, don't say no one told you. You don't have a home, or own a cow or a chicken or even a cat, like other young men of your age. What sort of man are you? A home is all I am asking for. When did the headman say he is now selling places for a home? They are given free. If only you cared ... (now I cannot hear her words. She is already crying.)

Tears are already dripping from mother's eyes. She is shaking and I cannot hear her words clearly enough. She is like one choking with something big on her throat, sobbing like a child. She cannot tell me the words coming from her heart any more. She is saying with her hands something I cannot understand. Maybe she does not want to say too many heavy words to you.

If only you could do as she says. You know how she gets thinner and thinner once this crying starts.

I will go back to school soon. I hope you will write me to tell me all these things she is talking about.

I hope you are well.

Your brother Mucha.

That night, the children huddled together in their sleep, boys and girls, faces soaked in tears. They felt the warmth of the coldness of the earth on their bodies and remembered that for the first time they would miss each other in days to come. The last night of the old homestead had arrived, like an unwanted visitor. There would be many more homes to which they would belong without asking any questions about them. The dreams to come, no one knew under which roof they would dream which dreams. Or under what sky, or shadow of what tree they would stand and think of the days to come.

The last night of their stay at the farm did not bring any dreams. It was no time for dreaming. They simply huddled together, boys and girls. Not quite boys some of them, but young men old enough to impregnate a woman. The girls were younger and small, tiny, with no ideas of their own about serious matters. Sisters and brothers, though. No one came to say farewell to them. It was only their hearts which said once more farewell to the birds and animals whose songs and yearnings they had hardly learnt to understand. They had helped the children to grow up, without telling them any of the secrets of their joys and sorrows.

No one came to whisper to them that there was love somewhere in the hearts of those remaining. No one. Not even a shadow walked past the cow-dung-covered doorstep to say farewell, May you go well. Nothing. For no one knew where these children were going. A farewell from anyone would have been an insult to them. How do you give a farewell to someone who does not even have a destination? Hence the cloud of silence. No voices dared to pile insult upon insult on the heads and hearts of the children.

Sleep would have come had someone told them where they were going to sleep the following night. Or how they were going to walk away from the homestead of their own father and tell anyone who saw them walk that they had to leave their own father. He did not want them any more. How could they tell anyone such stories?

The girls and the younger boy cried the whole night, sobbing and wondering what their homeless elder brothers would do for them, since they looked up to them for life, not death.

'If you cry, it makes the pain worse,' Jairosi, the biggest of the brothers, whispered to them in the middle of the night. No one was sure where the pain of their bodies was. At times it seemed all over the flesh, and at other times it seemed nowhere but everywhere with its namelessness. The tears too were all over the bodies of the children.

Maybe Jairosi was crying too, or at least sobbing his farewell to the land he had ploughed with his hands for many years. He felt it, too, in the soles of his feet and in the heartbeat which the land had given him. The land whose dark-brown soil clung to him like a second skin. The smell of the soil was also his smell. He cried for it with his heart. He could talk with other soils elsewhere, but the thought of the last word with the soil of his dreams was too much for him. This soil breathed the same breath as he breathed. When he spoke to it, the soil understood and answered back in words whose meaning he knew. It was the only soil for which he had given away everything. His life and his death he shared with it. Even the insects and plants of the land had become part of him. Their songs and colour, the cicadas' shrieky voices and the gleam of the blades of the leaves of the green maize, the bolls of the cotton plants fluffy and waving to the wind, the *mupani* trees clinging to the landscape like hardened fighters, they were all part of him.

Then he cried loudly. The other boys had hidden their tears as they hid themselves from the soul of the soil by going to school in far-away places. School had taken them from the land. They could not feel it in the same way Jairosi did. He had never gone to any of those far-away places, to escape. No. He had been here all the time, seeing the birds building nests and laying eggs before the nestlings came, seeing the little maize and cotton seeds explode in a forest of crops that one sold and made a fortune from. Everything had happened in his eyes. But now life had changed.

They had arrived here when they were young, some as babies, others as fragile boys and girls, whose only voice lay in the songs they had sung as they tried to herd the cattle in this valley of wild beasts and tall grass that covered both beast and person. Wide rivers, huge trees whose bellies surpassed the bellies of the fattest men they had ever seen, a profusion of animals in the forests, choruses of birds that greeted them with harsh messages of hatred and love. All of them had been young then, but full of fear and comfort at the same time. At least there had been their mother and father, brothers and sisters too, in this far-away place. A place too distant even for memory to travel to.

Now they had to move on again, divorced from the world they had learnt to accept. Their own father casting them away like a snake leaving its old skin for a new one. Their father had dreamt so many things on their behalf, they thought. They had heard him offer prayers to the ancestors, to the gods, asking them to protect them all, to take care of this blood which could spill so painfully in these lands of Gotami.

They felt their father cut tiny incisions in the palms of their hands and feet, rubbing powdered herbs in them, telling their ears that these herbs protected them from vicious snakes of this wild land of Gotami, snakes which obeyed the voice of the land. If you insult the ancestors of the land, even by mistake, snakes, monkeys, the soul of the soil, they get angry with you, Gotami's people had warned.

Respect the shrines of the land, the elders had said, and their father had taught them in his own words, day and night, every day. Thou shalt not. Thou shalt not. Thou shalt not. For ever. Until the fiftieth commandment of the land handed down from lip to lip in this land of shrines. The hills of their youthful memories did not smile at them any more that morning. It was time they walked away and not look back and admire what was not their own. The hills carried above them a certain smoky sadness, like a drowsy air. It was as if they wanted to send an onlooker's eye to sleep.

They missed the voices of the animals they had talked with in the wide forests. The squirrels, the *kudus*, the jackals which stole a small goat every now and then, the hyenas which howled at night. They would not hear them again with the same echoes of the hills and the rivers.

For years they had gone fishing in the big and sandy river. The smell of wet sand and fish still lingered in their noses. At the end of a fishing day, they had dangled tiny fish from their fishing hooks. Sometimes they had a small net, and if they ignored the sharp-toothed crocodiles, they plunged into the deep end of the pools and came out with vicious tiger-fish entangled in the nets. Then their fathers and mothers praised them, reciting the stories of the victories and failures of their ancestors. The wars won and the wars lost. They felt a little fire of pride burning inside them, their hearts glowing with a hidden pride kindled by the words of praise.

But now it was another story. Their hearts had to learn to yearn for another land which they did not know. They would reach it, maybe today or tomorrow or next week. They would get there, they thought. Every traveller arrives somehow. Inquiring along the way, getting lost, finding the way again, singing happily or sorrowfully, they would get there. You cannot get lost in the villages. A person who has a mouth cannot get lost. They would find the place one day. Walk on ahead. It is useless to think of the hills and fish and animals of the old homestead. Life or death is ahead. The cloud in the sky will be down on earth one day, as a mist or rain seeping into the soil. The eagle might fly high, but it will perch one day. It will surely perch. Walk on, plod on, to the very end. The journey never ends. It is the traveller who ends.

This journey started long ago, years back, when they sat and heard John White and Ngwarumapundu singing the sorrow of migration in the fourth-class coach of the crowded train. 'Pack your things, everybody,' their father had ordered them. 'The train will leave tonight, with you and everybody else,' he had said. That was after he had taken the women and little children first to far-away places. He returned after what seemed endless weeks. The bigger children would not have to go, he said, those who could carry their own bags.

They remembered the night at the station, cold and subdued as if they were being taken to prison. No one talked about anything else except stories of how some strong and angry men threw smaller men out of the windows of the train. How the strong men were feared. How the strong men were feared even by the policemen. Or the stories of how ignorant travellers were lured into getting off at the wrong stations and were then robbed by thieves who waited there for such misfortunes.

In the train John White was there, charging sixpence for his music. If they had a little more money left after buying the buns, which smelled like perfume, they would ask John White to play a song for them. A song or two. That might help them forget the land of their birth which they had left behind them. Forget the donkeys which kicked at them and scarred their foreheads and knees, the big bulls whose horns they secretly sharpened so they would not shame them when they engaged bulls from a neighbouring herd, the little goats they carelessly castrated without caring about the noise they made as they shouted for help. The voices of the bleating sheep. There were games, too, of the slippery *nhanzva* tree, which they rode down the slopes of the hills, slithering on the rocks like giant snakes. The music might make them forget all this, opening their hearts to the new land of new folktales.

'Children travelling half-ticket? What has that to do with me? Do they hear half the music?' John White, the albino, had protested as they sat in the crowded coach, heading for the unknown. Fanwell, their brother, had wanted to pay John White half the price of each piece of music. It was the children who paid, he said. Children travelled half-ticket on the train, so they could have everything at half the price, his logic went. The singer would have none of that. There was nothing like half an ear, John White laughed, sometimes sweetening his words with his talking wires. '*Ndizvozvo!*' the strains of his wires said, evoking laughter and wonder from the travellers. Everyone wondered how he made the wires talk. Was it the little bottle with many-coloured substances inside it? As soon as the wires spoke, all was forgotten and forgiven. The noise of the train was soon lost to the ear, drowned by the talking guitar and the wailing voice of the singer. Destination: the unknown city of cotton, the place of dwarfish ghosts, the hearts of the children said, afraid.

'*Ndapedza!*' 'I have finished!' the talking wires said at the end of the song, the owner of the guitar moving on along the rows and rows of travellers, some of whom talked about their travels while others sang the songs of their distant homes, drinking if they had something to quench their thirst with.

Behind them was the place where the umbilical cords had been buried the day each one of them was born. The yells of their births were there too, with the sun which rose from above the trees and hills they knew well, and then set behind the hills and trees they had grown up nursing. Even in their sleep, they knew where their heads would be on the sleeping mat without having to be told. All those worries stirred their heads and hearts. Gatooma, they thought in the silence of their hearts.

Everything was behind them now, including goats and sheep whose colours they knew from the colours of the fathering he-goats and sows. The echoes of voices from familiar hills, the little friends who were not so little, and the village witches who threatened their nightly sleep, the village drunks too, who sang all the vulgar words and deeds, dancing their way home in the dark – they would miss them. They would miss the old women's voices when the night came and they sang about the mischief of men and women of the village at the beer party. Even the ghosts hiding in the anthills and the rivers: they would miss them. Their hearts had now been torn away from the soil which was in their veins.

There were doves too which cooed in familiar tones from the giant *musasa* trees under which the children had played the games of guessing which pod would explode next, and how many seeds would scatter where, drawing circles in the sand with their dirty fingers and toes.

All was behind them. They were like escapees from a land of the past to an emptiness of the future. All left behind because a man, their father, had slept and dreamt. They only hoped this dream would not be a nightmare.

Already, as the train trudged on, they saw themselves writing letters to friends left behind in the forgotten world of their birth, letters about how the sun had already begun to play tricks on us, how the rivers flowed in the wrong direction, how the people of Gotami's lands spoke like children, and how the cattle died after being bitten by insects as large as doves, large insects called tsetse flies, which everyone talked about although no one ever claimed to have seen. Letters about the roar of the lions in our sleep. Do you know that the roar of a lion can make a whole hut crumble and fall to pieces? But, oh, how I miss the games we used to play under the large *muonde* tree. In this new place, there are no uncles or aunts. Strange place, this. The people of Gotami, they call many things in queer ways. How can a man say *nangara* when he means 'look', *tarira*? They make you laugh when they say *yahwe* instead of simply saying *iwe*. They are strange people, though. They do not even tell you what those words mean. You have to keep on guessing and guessing. Maybe that is why the white man forced them to move to places beyond the mountains.

Ah, they would write back, how shameful it was that I was on the train, listening to Ngwarumapundu and John White and Jacob Mhungu, without shoes on my feet! Do you remember those voices from your uncle's small radio? The one we listened to during the night? Yes, Ngwarumapundu and John White, I saw them. I heard them sing on the train. Sitting barefoot on the carriage bench, like a dog. Everyone else had shoes except me and my brothers and sisters. To take a train without shoes on! To smell the glory of the city with bare feet down there, licking the hard Tarmac road! It was embarrassing. I felt sorry for myself, the letter went on. It was a shame. Like waking up to find that your wet dreams of last night were only urine all over the sleeping mat, with your sisters standing there as you wake up, teasing you, denouncing all your yesterday's boastfulness about beards and fatherhood at the *mahumbwe* games. I will tell you more about this land of Gotami. I will have to go and herd the goats and sheep. Otherwise father will shout at me if I lose them and they are killed by greedy hyenas. I don't even know how I will send this letter. There are no schools or people who come with letters in this place, the voices of the letters said.

PS. After two weeks, there is nowhere to post this letter.

Chinya mutondo baba vabaya n'ombe yashe,
Chinya mutondo vakasiya mharapara yoga,
Chinya mutondo baba vabaya n'ombe yashe,
Chinya mutondo vakasiya mharapara yoga,
Iwe itawo ndiitewo!

Are you still singing the song? How we sang it together the day before we left! It is hard in this new land to find someone to sing our songs with. And you can't even see the moon. The trees are so big. The grass is tall. We cannot play outside. Father says the lions are looking for anyone of us who strays from the others. Imagine, when we want to relieve ourselves at night, we have to ask some big person to accompany us.

That was years back. No one wanted to remember those days of elephants and hyenas in the homestead, sharing life with human beings. The days were different now. A new moon had been born. Red as a fire.

'Where are we going?' the elder girl cried, tears seeping out of her eyes, bewildered by it all. No one answered her. No one knew where the journey would end.

'Behind those blue hills,' a voice said, not quite sure itself where the blue hills were and what made them blue when other hills were green with the leaves of happy trees. 'That's where they say *mukoma* Fanwell's new home is,' the voice goes on.

From that day, the children would only know their

new home as Beyond-the-Hills. Far away in a place which turns hills smoky-blue. A place of no echoes.

Fanwell hears voices of people he does not know. He stands up and walks to the footpath to look. All he can see are shapes of people who are not sure of the way they have taken. They speak in undertones, sometimes arguing, at times laughing. Someone seems to know what he wants them to do. This way. The footpath is difficult at night, he hears.

'We are almost there,' a drunken voice says. 'I know your brother and his wife. You know he has a wife? They just came to settle here and found some of us already in the battle to keep the elephants from our fields at night. We'll manage somehow.'

Fanwell hears a familiar voice. Soon, he is crying, embracing the little girls and the bigger boys. There is pain in his heart. His young wife, almost a girl, does not know what to do. She stands there without a word. The girls cry too. They are tired and worn out. Were it not for the stranger they met along the footpath, they would have slept in the forest, the girls say, in between tears.

The boys too are crying. They do not want to remember the story of their journey. But Fanwell insists they must tell it. He wants to know. How does he tell his wife if you do not tell him what happened? You tell him that he already knows but he does not want to think he knows. He wants to hear the story again.

'Where is mother?' he asks.

'She went a long time ago. They say she will be here any time. She went to see her own people, to tell them what happened. She will come here soon,' Jairosi, the short one, tells him.

Fanwell sits down and rekindles the fire. He does not have words any more. All he can do is watch the little tongue-like flames flapping in the night like the wings of a tired bat. The silence that descends on his face also descends on the faces of the children. It is enough. Why speak words when this silence can tell it all? He looks at this one hut and worries where these children will sleep. What will they eat? This journey has ended in a dark cave, he thinks.

You look at Fanwell and feel pity for him. Time has not been good to him. Burdens like this kill, you think. Burdens.

After many days, Fanwell points at the soil and says: This is our salvation. We have to work the soil so you children can go to school. I know that no one is going to starve to death. That I know for sure. We might sleep on an empty stomach one day or so, but we will survive.

He talks on and on, to himself, to everybody, to nobody. Tears gather on his ageing face. He wipes them away so he can seem strong. He talks and talks, telling stories of so many things which he has seen and heard. He talks and talks until he forgets that there is no one listening. Everyone is sleeping now. There is the sound of someone snoring. Someone releasing an unguarded fart.

Fanwell still talks on and on. Snore or fart, he talks and talks on like an everlasting echo. His voice is gentle at times, harsh and tearful at others. A mixture of anger and desperation. He is calling to you, urging you to come up this hill . . . right up here, to a cave. Listen to the whoo-whoo-bird's voice coming from the rocks. These leafy trees, they were here before your fathers were born. Even before your ancestors were born they were here. In these caves are the snails, the silent ones, the lizards whose tails sweep the faces of the rocks, the rock rabbits which are occasionally ambushed and constricted by the pythons and swallowed whole while you sleep in the comfort of your mother's hut. The eagles too, from the sky, see these things when the sun shines and wonder why the Creator did not give rock rabbits the power of the wing. Wings, they are weapons of both escape and attack.

You walk with Miriro through the night, into the early hours of the morning, tracing a path only she knows how to discern. A dark path, an invisible path, which frightens you. She has been here, she says through Fanwell's voice. The person who walks along the footpath across the rock without faltering has surely walked there before. Miriro walks along in the semi-darkness, her eyes fixed on the familiar pebbles which she will use as the marks of the old path she walked before you were born.

'Come along. Don't be tired.' You hear her urging voice. She will urge you again, on and on, to see the hills which she has wanted to show to someone who would be born long after she is dead. The woman tells you that your chest is weak. It cannot contain the hard words and experiences which she wants to show you. But some way must be found to strengthen it. A man whose heart cannot contain heavy burdens in silence has a weak chest. She knows you are young and should not be burdened with such stories. An older member of the family should have been chosen. Not you. Your knees are weak too. A weak heart and weak knees. You are afraid. Your heart wants to explode. You can hear the echoes of its throb from the caves of the hills. Throb throb throb. A leaf flies by in the half-darkness, nibbling at your face like the tongue of some ominous snake. A long-winged bird flaps away from your face, startled by this nocturnal visit. Another sound of the shrinking night, a sound whose source you can never guess.

Whispers and their echoes. The dead speak. Ghostly shapes in this dying night, half-dark, half-light. A dark silence embraces you. Maybe it is your heart, or Miriro's, throbbing wildly, you don't know any more.

She takes you by the hand like a blind child. Her ageing grip is stronger all the time, giving you the confidence of her many years of walking these parts. She stops behind a single boulder. The squirrels shout to each other a warning about your arrival. Enemy! Enemy! they shout. Beware you who dwell in our realm, they shout. They are on top of the rocks and inside invisible caves, warning their young ones and the pregnant mothers to run. The snakes too know there are intruders in the night.

The trees are whispering to us as their leaves rub shoulders in the cool breeze from the east. Why do all winds come from the east? you wonder. The rains and rain clouds are dragged from the east. The cold air is also dragged from the east. You are already thinking about the winds of death, from the east where all the other winds come from. Your mind is dizzied by all these things that pile up in your heart, already burdened by so many other dreams and nightmares.

Miriro looks at you as at a small child. You take courage in the fact that she has not left you standing there to go into the caves. She is with you. She stands there, with you, her hands on your shoulders.

'One day, a man came here wielding a knife.' Miriro points at a shallow cave. 'He came here and waited for herdboys. The knife scraped the sides of a rock without getting blunt. He lay here the whole day, morning, afternoon, evening, waiting. He waited for the one he wanted to kill. He would not kill anyone else. It had to be someone chosen by the herbalists.

'The man, tall and wearing eyes without mercy, waited and hoped that his ancestors would not let him down. He breathed deeply and half-coughed, his pulse wild with what he was about to do. It was getting dark, and the children had to collect the cattle and drive them back to their parents. The man's last moments in hiding would be in vain. His eyes kept watching the stray cows to see who would follow them, the little feet that would climb there to pursue the cows. He waited and waited. No child came. It was supposed to be a boy, the first-born or the last-born.

'When it was getting too dark, the man left. I will come again tomorrow, another day, he said. One day is not enough to cause fresh meat to go bad. A dream cannot be said to be serious unless it haunts the dreamer for several days, he said, and walked away, sad that the wealth promised him as reward for the human sacrifice had melted away, for once, before his very eyes.

'A poor man, he knew that if he played with the rich, his poverty could be converted to wealth. From the time he was young, he had told his children that they should play with the children of the rich. You never know what herbs their parents rub on their bodies. They might rub some on to your bodies and your life will change. The man went home and slumped on his wooden stool, his head dropping near the fireplace where his wife cooked and sang songs about endless poverty and a man who wore weakness as his shoes. If a child of his homestead falls sick, it is because of the herbs it is stuffed with. If a goat of this homestead falls sick, it is because of the herbs I am stuffed with. But when the children and wives of others fall sick, they see the white man's hospital and a nurse in pure white.

'Early the following morning Tsapi, the rich medicine-man, walked to the man's homestead. He wore strong tyre sandals which everyone in the village feared and respected. Early in the morning, before the sun had time to think of leaving its mother of fires, Tsapi was there, whispering to the messenger of death.

'"Did you do as you promised?" Tsapi asked the man, his voice harsh and remote, like one speaking to someone across the river.

'The man pleaded his failure, sad that wealth seemed to escape him every time it was on his doorstep, crying, weeping like a child.

'The next day, your father was at Tsapi's homestead,

riding a shiny bicycle. Tsapi greeted your father and laughed about a man not destined to enjoy wealth. "You see, my friend," Tsapi laughed, "every day wealth filters through your fingers like sand." Tsapi laughed at your father.

'That was the day when dreams of far-away places started . . .' Fanwell talks on and on, for years and years, through your dreams and nightmares. What use is silence? He will talk to you about these things and what they mean. He will sing about them with his friends and wish he had never known about them. He will not feel bad about them all the time, thinking that to feel bad about these things is also to accept the defeat of time, to carry love and hatred in the same heart. Water and fire in the same pot.

In the playground, the children swarmed the drawn circle, each ready to sing the songs that were in the air. They sang and clapped their hands, their small feet pattering on the hard soil. Half-naked, with torn pants and old vests for shirts, they sang and danced. No one else was looking. No one heard what they sang about themselves.

> When I grow up,
> I will . . .
> When I grow up,
> I will . . .
> When I grow up,
> I will . . .

They went on. Their voices echoed in the caves of the nearby hill. There were teachers, nurses, priests, LDOs, mechanics. Everyone was there. Once they said they were going to be teachers, then you saw a teacher in the little one, walking with the authority of Teacher, biting a stick for a cigarette. The girls running after Teacher, carrying his books to his house. Teacher sits on the chair of his house and marks books.

The LDO too is important. He walks with the power of life and death. He whistles as he thinks about whether the rains will fall this year. The goats and the sheep, bring them for castration. The small bulls, bring them for de-horning. All those are brought. The man does not hold a single bull by the horns. He instructs others to do it, to hold there, to cut there, to put a black powder on the scar of the small bull. He is the LDO, a white man who must not touch dirt.

No one likes the priest. He wants children to come for Sunday school when parents want them to go herding cattle. The priest and the teacher are friends. The priest sends the names of those who do not come to Sunday school to the teacher on Monday. When the children are caned, the priest looks at their bleeding buttocks in feigned pain. His face pretends he does not like to see children suffering under the weight of the cane. But everyone knows it is the priest who sent the names of those who did not attend Sunday school.

So anyone who says they want to be a priest becomes an enemy of the children. But still they let him act out the life of a priest. Most of the children laugh at the priest. What school did he go to? they ask. No one has ever heard what school the priest went to. They burst out in laughter. Leave him, they say.

Then comes the dip-tank attendant, harsh and angry. He threatens all the time. If you do not do this or that, your cattle will not go into the dip tank. The child acting attendant is full of airs. He stands on a brick, calling out the names of the owners of the cattle, ordering them to drive their cattle into the dip tank or else!

The children's games are going to be long today. So many children. So many games to play, the new ones especially. The new ones of the children who are already in school, and those who have been to the city of lights and death by knife-stabbing. Let us play until we are tired, the children remind themselves.

You remember all those games you played, many years ago. Now you look at Fanwell. You look at yourself and your brothers. You think that you should not have wasted time telling them, 'When I grow up I want to become a teacher or LDO or priest.' You look at the despairing faces of everyone, Fanwell, Jairosi and the younger ones. You want to say: When I grow up, I want to die! but the voice sticks in your throat. You swallow some saliva to soothe your throat. Still no words come out. You hear a voice shouting but it is not heard by anyone else: When I grow up, I want to go far away from this place, this place of hatred. When I grow up, I want to have nothing to do with the dream of Gotami's lands. You hear the voice and it makes you cry. You see the picture of your mother and know that this land is cruel. You cry in your sleep. You cry when you wake up. You cry as you walk to the bush to relieve yourself. Every place is the place of tears. Every tree's shade is the shade of tears. You wait for the day when there will be no tears around you. In your mind you know that such a day has still to be created.

The echoes of the voice of your youth become more painful. When I grow up, I will . . . I will . . .

Die.

It is not long before your mother comes back from her own people. She has never talked much about them. It is as if they never existed. An orphan given away in a marriage, and then taken over by another one she did not believe in. They let her go through all that. Now she behaves as if they did not exist. Or is it dangerous for them to exist? None of you knows why, but she does not talk much about her people.

Today her face is full of a new, calm happiness. You look at her. She stares back at you. Whenever she does this, staring at you with an eye loaded with questions, you think about stories you have not told her. You feel the weight of her eye on your heart. You feel your heart beating to her blinking. Why did I not tell her some of these things? you think. You have not told her that many years ago, alone, you took a bus on a Saturday morning from the city, early in the morning, before anyone else woke up in the college where you were. War was all over the place. A friend had warned you that you could easily die if you walked into the areas where guerrillas were fighting the white man to free our land. Don't walk into death with your eyes wide open, he had warned you.

But you refused to hear his words. Death will come anyway, one way or the other. 'There is one piece of land which I want to see,' you told your friend. He had felt what you felt, especially the sadness of your dreams and how you talked at night and mentioned names he did not know.

'I will come with you,' your friend had said, looking at you through his dark glasses. You got on the bus in silence, hearing the urging of voices you did not understand.

'Yes, you are the grandson of an interesting man. A great man, that one,' an old man had told you when you got to the place you wanted to see. 'He carved this stool for my father when I was young. He carved a drum. I cannot play it now. All the songs are gone. It was carved by holy hands, beautiful hands of a great man,' the old man went on, telling you stories of how he had admired your grandfather and dreamt that one day he too would get to know him better before he died. How he heard stories about your grandfather making rain, summoning clouds at will in the middle of the dry season, playing his drum to the tune of his voice while perched up a tree like an eagle, his voice flooding the hills and the valleys, long before the white man took away the land and defiled the holy shrines of our pride.

You become more intimate with the man now. You ask him where the grave of your grandfather is. Only tears, a stream of tears from the eyes of the man, greet you. He searches for ways to change the subject. To soothe you out of what you have come in search of, as if you have been searching for your death, for the pain of knowing. Pain is stored in the stories of the land since the beginning of time.

In the midst of the tears, a shrieky, tearful voice sprouts like a plant from a dying seed, slowly. 'Your grandfather's grave, they removed it and threw away the bones. They were making that road there, with bulldozers.' The old man is silent after that, his finger pointing in a permanent gesture in the direction of a cluster of trees where a road passes through.

You are silent in your own tears, seeing the bones of your own blood scattered in the plains, in the valleys, in the hills, playthings for children. Death, hatred, they meet inside you. They are too big for words. The pain takes your heart away, on endless journeys.

As you walk away, the old man takes your hand, just to shake it. He looks the other way as if you and your friend were apparitions parting with him. The deep silence of tears tells you that you are children of pity. 'I am a child of pity,' you whisper inside yourself. Tears. Tears, and more tears. Pain. Feet touch the soil without touching the soul of the pebbles. You walk away from pain . . .

Your mother sits there still, looking at your withered face that has been taken away by this reverie. You have never told her this story. It is a story only you will know, you think. Her eye accuses you of what both of you know, each in the silence of their own heart.

'I always thought I should talk to you,' she says, her words floating slowly through the dry air. 'You and your younger brother are angry. You wear hearts of anger. Your brother does not search for knowledge to put into the fire of his anger. You search for stories and knowledge to fuel your anger. It is a bad type of anger. You search for things that makes you angrier. Soon it will turn to hatred. Hatred eats into you,' she says. And when I want to ask her what her words mean, she gestures to keep me silent. 'You see, you dream all sorts of things. Fireflies and birds, flying and perching. You dream. I warned you not to run after the fireflies of your dreams. They may have real flames which can burn your days. Is it not true that you went to the graves of your fathers to see them? Don't answer me. You were turning your anger into hatred.' You hear her words echoing in your heart.

'Yes, so you did not go to your people. You went to the grave of my grandfather. An old man met you and told you I had been there many years before.' You feel betrayed.

Your mother does not want to speak. She fears words might burn your anger into hatred, she says. You were too young to know, but it is time for you to know now. A man marries a woman. He dies. The woman is inherited by another relative. The children of the woman continue to be children of the one who died. That is your story. You have seen the place of the grave of your father. 'The hatred of the way things have been must now stop.' She starts to cry. She is like a young girl who has spilled a gourd of water at the doorstep. You hear her voice long after she has spoken. The hills and mountains of your growing up, the songs and the dances, all become different. The games of naming. The love songs in the children's playground. The tales of animals and gods, they are now new in your ears. The voices that accompanied you through your life change into distant echoes with different meanings in them. You look at her and see a new face, a silent face, which hid everything from you all these years because you were young. Fresh like a brittle leaf. Young. The echo of her voice refuses to leave your sleep, your waking days. You are different.

As she takes a handful of grain and throws it into the wind, the birds sing a different song to you. She throws some of it on your head, with incantations and chants. Inside you a smile flickers like a little flame with no ashes any more. 'This anger which could burn is dead now.' You hear her over and over again.

198 –

The dead live as mere echoes of songs long-vanished, dreams. They part with the living, abandoning all they yearned for while they lived. Wealth, smiling friends with white teeth and red gums, blooming flowers which they dared not see while their eyes flashed with light. They walk away in the dark, in the early-morning light or the coolness of an impending night. Cool hours when elders sit to talk important matters of the village. Hours when birds sing as they watch the ticklish bodies of children bathing at the river, tired and naked bodies of alert women who will always ask: Is there someone coming? We are bathing. Please cross the river by another crossing place. And the, oh yes, we are sorry, we did not know there were women bathing, of a male voice behind the rocks, feigning that no male eyes have feasted on the shape of a female body glittering with the river water.

The night before, an owl had perched on the roof of one of the huts, right on top. He sat there and hooted, the echo of his voice reaching far into the dark night. No one dared throw a stone at him. They only lit bundles of dry grass and saw him fly away in the darkness like a shadow. When darkness returned, they heard him hoot again in his endless chorus. Who-whoo! Who-whoo! Who-whoo! Then another bundle of dry grass in the flames. Flapping wings in the dark. Ghosts cannot be mentioned by name in the dark. They will appear, walking on two legs, to announce their presence.

'What is it?' the sick man wants to know.

'It's nothing,' the woman sitting next to his sick-bed answers.

'Leave it there. I know what it wants,' the sick man goes on, his voice now feeble, faint, words coming out of his mouth in small trickles. The smoke of a dying fire. Not a word in answer to his own. The eyes of the other women by the bed swerve this way and that, near and far, searching for each other's faces in the semi-darkness. The game of eyes stops. The night seems to stop too.

At last your father lay there, like a baby born deaf and

dumb, waiting. His face worn out, dry with the pain inside his body. You had not seen him for many years. The years of anger. When last you saw him, he had stood there, silhouetted against the maize fields like a soldier ready for battle.

'You did well to come,' he said to you, adding in a faint whisper, 'Anger should not last forever.' You stared at him without words on your lips. Only the rusty words worn out with time remained, the rusty anger that had piled in your body like coals of invisible fires.

In the tense silence of the room, he held your hand in his. You felt the coldness of his body and tears trickled out of your eyes. Your eyes avoided his. You did not want him to see the tears from your eyes. It would pain him more, knowing that you had seen death in his eyes and felt it in his cold pulse. The silence would last for an endless period, like the time when a thorn is stuck into our flesh and someone is trying to remove it, but you feel the pain amassing itself in your whole body, killing you without killing you, burning your body like a massive flame. In such moments, the blink of an eye becomes a whole year.

When you walk out of the room, people are sitting outside, by the door, resigned like passengers waiting for a bus that does not come. Old women and men, a child or two running after their playthings, young women whose voices sharpen themselves for a wail, men who smoke paper-rolled cigarettes and pretend to like them. Everybody is there.

'It should not take this long,' a voice said.

'It is better to die than to continue in this pain,' another says.

You hear it and want to continue holding your father's hand. You want to hold his hand, to stop him from taking this long journey beyond Gotami's lands. You want to feel his pulse in your pulse, to share the heartbeat which you have with him, so he can hold on to his old dream.

Already you see the faces of people around you not feeling the pain any more. They wait for his death. They wait for many other things which they know his death will give them. Those who know how to whisper are already calling each other to come outside in order to whisper into ears. Come, we will be back in a short while. Come, I would like to share a few words with you. Come, can we see each other in a quiet place? Come, I have been looking for you for a while.

A year after your father's death, you sit by a glowing night fire, listening to old songs that soar into the air like migratory birds. Old words that move old and young hearts. Old tunes which vibrate the hearts and souls of caves and shrines. The songs come and go in waves as dancers and singers take away tunes and words from each other, giving them back to where they came from, and then taking them back again, as if the music is on a swing. Words shift from mouth to mouth, all soaring into the air like myriads of fish-eagles flooding the sky, tearing it apart before putting it back together again with their graceful wings. The songs become echoes from a distant mountain, going and coming, spreading into hearts and into the blood of hearers and singers.

The dancers crack their soles with the dance. The earth becomes one with the flesh possessed by the dance. Drums and rattles are warm today. The bare soles of the dancers are warm too. You can feel the hot skins of their palms every time you shake hands with them. Some are cracking, others are blistered.

Voices float in the night air, taking with them warm saliva and hot air. Every throat discovers that it is not only for swallowing and breathing. The voices swell in the night air, breaking the power of the wind and the night.

You feel in your heart that this night will not end. Night and day are married together in this celebration. Voices drown the night and the day. Song silences the itching throat of the cockerel, stopping him from singing his daily song of the coming of a new day. He feels overpowered and so resigns to a surprised silence.

As you doze off, carried away on the wings of song and dance, you see a flame that spreads over the old homestead, engulfing the people and the trees like a thick mist. 'Look, that's the flame,' a voice whispers to you. You search for the owner of the voice everywhere. You open granaries and houses, but the owner of the voice is not there. You sing with the singers and dance with the dancers of the ritual, but the owner of the voice is not among them.

From far away in the sky, where the flame is spreading,

the voice still shouts faintly, like the voice of a child. In your sleep the flame still spreads like an endless mat. With every word that is sung, every foot that draws dance patterns on the ground, the flame spreads on and on, a mist drifting away in the wind, an endless woollen blanket so light the wind carries it away effortlessly.

Tariro too is drifting with the woollen blanket of a flame. Ever since she returned after her sojourn in the land of the unknown tongues, she has not belonged here. Her soul is absent. Bitter words come out of her mouth, but she calms herself and walks away. All the time she feels bitterness in her heart.

She is walking on the cloud of flames. It is pointless for her to try to put the flames out, such a vast flame that embraces the whole sky above the homestead. Even when she calls Miriro, the silent one, for help, Miriro looks the other way. She is deaf to this new destiny. She is blind too. Words refuse to come out of her own mouth. The new dance is out of her reach.

Miriro whispers something to Tariro. The two are silent for a while, almost like statues. They have no words or movement of any sort. Frozen, as if they have become corpses.

Then Tariro, the younger of the two, walks away. Shortly, she brings a young girl with breasts as tiny as the tip of a thin woman's finger. The girl kneels beside the elder women to give them respect. Miriro holds her by the hand and puts a large shiny coin in the girl's palm. The young girl walks away to the edge of the flame cloud, drops the shiny coin into a large hole where lizards and salamanders live. They will eat it, she thinks. They will eat it one day, her inner voice says, as she walks towards the two elder women without turning her head. She walks with a stiff neck, not turning, not gesturing to tempt back the shiny coin.

'Maybe the flame that burns the homestead will die after this.' You hear Miriro's words from far away. She is there, pointing away from the homestead, her words getting fainter and fainter, feeble like the words of a dying old man. As her voice dies, you see her face fading too. Tariro, too, is fading. She refuses to look at the homestead which gave her away like a goat at the market place. The two walk from this land of ancestors in which they have lived with tears in their eyes and burdens in their hearts.

Still the cockerel does not crow. You can hear only echoes of its voice in the distance. The night has taken its voice away. The bird will be silent for another long night, its wings drab and its feathers floating on the wind and burning in the flame embracing this home. The little flames of the fireflies will be dead also, blown by this wind which carries away even dreams of women, men, children and fireflies.